# Hitman from Hell

God rules Heaven.
Satan rules Hell.
The Godfather rules the Bronx.

Trel W. Sidoruk

This is a work of fiction. Names, characters, businesses, places, events and incidents are either the products of the author's imagination and/or used in a fictitious manner. Any resemblance to actual persons, living or dead, places, or actual events is purely coincidental.

Copyright 2017 – All rights reserved to Trel W. Sidoruk

Published by Mo Peanuts

***Your Dream, Our Team, Full Steam!***

www.MoPeanuts.com

ISBN: 978-0-9971513-3-6

# Hitman From Hell

Written by Trel W. Sidoruk

Edited by Lauren Sidoruk

Illustrated by Aleksandra Klepacka

# DEDICATION

*To all the vicious freaks that rattled my cage...*

*Thank you for freeing the beast.*

# TABLE OF CONTENTS

| | |
|---|---|
| Chapter 1 | Limping on Empty |
| Chapter 2 | Dressing on the Side |
| Chapter 3 | Close Quarters |
| Chapter 4 | A Name by No Other |
| Chapter 5 | Partners in Crime |
| Chapter 6 | Risky Rendezvous |
| Chapter 7 | From Bad to Evil |
| Chapter 8 | Dunlop's Debut |
| Chapter 9 | Cleanup in Aisle 5 |
| Chapter 10 | Doubling Down |
| Chapter 11 | Listen or Go Deaf |
| Chapter 12 | The Hunt Begins |
| Chapter 13 | Pro Ho on the Go |
| Chapter 14 | Criminal Commitment |
| Chapter 15 | Joy Riding |
| Chapter 16 | Late for an Important Date |
| Chapter 17 | Get Ready, Get Set, Go! |
| Chapter 18 | Building Momentum |
| Chapter 19 | You Are What You Eat |
| Chapter 20 | Strange Bedfellows |
| Chapter 21 | From Unfolding to Unraveling |
| Chapter 22 | I Could Have Been a Contender |
| Chapter 23 | Long Time, No See |
| Chapter 24 | Deal with the Devil |
| Chapter 25 | I'm my Brother's Keeper |
| Chapter 26 | Three Paths, One Destination |
| Chapter 27 | A Touching Moment |

# Chapter 1

# Limping on Empty

As the silver 1987 Honda Civic Sedan putters through the campus gates and onto East Fordham Road, Professor Dunlop's cringe recesses slightly as the tailpipe clears the curb. Temporarily avoiding yet another jarring jolt, which would surely mean the destruction of yet another important piece to his commuting machine's cohesion, Dunlop finds himself once again appreciating the little things that had made the Civic one of the bestselling vehicles of all time.

Though the car was now less than a thousand miles from demolition, years earlier, the then-brand-new-ride had been affectionately christened the "Silver Bullet" by Dunlop's uncle. During his toast to his third favorite nephew, his uncle proclaimed the paint job the only thing at Dunlop's graduation party that could possible outshine his ascension in academia. The car was a gift from his proud parents, who boasted that due to his partial scholarship, more than enough money had been saved to make the purchase a much deserved no-brainer.

At his zenith, Dunlop grabbed life by the proverbial balls, graduating from SUNY Binghamton with honors, and subsequently green-lit for professorship at the college of his choosing. Professor Dunlop had plunged penis first into his field of choice like so many young men before him, falling in love with archaeology via the silver screen. From Tarzan to Indiana Jones, to the beautiful women who loved them both, archaeology was exciting, worldly, and romantic. Dabbling in politics and history, as well as having a myriad of sexy skills and astonishing attributes, an archaeologist was an occupation that kept the knife sharp and the fork full.

Dunlop had sprung at an opportunity for a professorship at Fordham University in the Bronx, where a position became available when an old colleague of his mentor retired. Landing the job with little more than a casual coffee in a campus eatery, Dunlop was on top of the world. Marrying his college sweetheart and producing intellectually superior children were prudent next steps. Everything was going smashingly well until a series of missteps caused his career to stumble. As with so many people, Dunlop loved to be loved, but his subpar self-worth and pitiful people skills were a bad recipe for someone who found himself in a position of power over people he longed to make love with.

A sexual harassment complaint filed by one of his star pupils had derailed his promising career, until an accusation from a fellow professor knocked him completely off-track and hurtling towards a darker destination. Caught literally with his pants down, Dunlop had feigned curiosity in hopes of persuading a powerful college alumni, who was also hiding deep within the walk-in closet of sexuality, to finance a dig in the jungles of Colombia, based on hearsay and a map that couldn't be authenticated. Once the board determined that Dunlop knew the facts to be no more than legend and lore, Dunlop was put on indefinite probation. Sensing it was only a matter of time before he was shown the door, he was desperate to make a name for himself, before his name became mud.

One way to make a name for yourself in archaeology is to make a landmark discovery. Careers are made on a single find, and Dunlop knew if he could just land the next big thing, his latest escapade would be considered anything but. Therefore, when he sold his soul to the Devil, it didn't seem like such a steep price to pay, considering he was already in professional purgatory, hoping for a quick decision either way. Of course, he hadn't actually made a pact with Satan, but rather with the Mob, who, at least in the beginning, when Dunlop could still float his debt, were surprisingly professional and personable. Things had only recently gone south since he'd misfired on a couple of surefire hits.

More jaded now than ever, Dunlop was shocked at the corruption that ran rampant throughout the most civilized of society's social circles. All he wanted to do was import objects of historical and/or religious significance, and put them in a place of higher learning for safe keeping and study. He was a servant of knowledge, a steward of sociology, an altruistic academic. He deserved to have his portrait hanging proudly on a wall in the college's library, not his back against a wall with his career hanging in the wind. In his self-righteously skewed view, he was trying to make the world a better place, selflessly assisting otherwise destitute native peoples of third-world countries by putting some greenbacks in their back pockets, so they could escape the savage jungle before it was sawed down in the name of progress.

But this? This world where everyone was trying to screw one another for no other reason than to notch their belts, frustrated Dunlop deeply. He'd sent money and performed favors for more unsavory characters in the past six months than he cared to remember. The money he'd sent in good faith was gone. The favors performed, unappreciated. The items that were supposed to come in return for payment, poof... The best showing to date was a cheaply crafted forgery of a Mayan king's brooch. A ping of pain crossed his smoked-stained smile whenever he revisited the moment he had opened the UPS box. Filled with so much wonder, so much joy... The world was Dunlop's oyster until he saw the made in China stamp on the gold-painted, recycled iron accessory, which had been billed as antiquities from Argentina, but in the end, was nothing more than accoutrement for a low-level officer's uniform in the People's Liberation Army.

Now grasping for straws instead of life's balls, he questions last month's answers that have yielded last place results. As he rides the bumper of the car in front of him, he rides himself, questioning the rearview mirror like it owes him money. "Where the fuck you been?!?! Trying to teach a summer course in hopes of getting back into his department's good graces is where!" Of course, Dunlop hadn't been able to show up all week due to a rendezvous in Canada that left him answering a border agent's questions, while a canine narcotics team ransacked his luggage. Looking for something they refused to tip their Stetsons to, the Royal Canadian Mounted Police came to a startling revelation… The Ming vase on which Dunlop had spent the remaining pittance of his pension, was, in fact, just a vase, no more valuable than one purchased legally in Bed, Bath & Beyond.

Reliving the life-crushing moment yet once again, Dunlop's throat constricts, as he regrets not choosing to go out in a blaze of glory, before the agents had a chance to laugh themselves off to an early lunch. Shooting the last of the Mounties with his imaginary machine gun, Dunlop is about to lay down a line from an 80's action film, when he's jolted from his long lapse of lucidity by a blaring cellphone ringtone. Discombobulated upon his unceremonious return to reality, Dunlop grazes the coffee cup that's precariously perched on the center console, when he flings his arm out to a pile of papers on his passenger seat that he plans to rifle through, in hopes of finding the phone before it goes dark.

Sadly, the strike to the Styrofoam cup was his most forceful in years, causing the cup to careen towards the passenger car seat.

When the coffee cup falls to the seat cushion, it doesn't just spill, it explodes, dousing his brown, worn, leather satchel along with every loose piece of paper in the car. Livid, Dunlop wails, "Fuck me!" Finally finding the phone, Dunlop frantically hits the answer button and clumsily flicks the phone on speaker before dropping it back on the pile of sodden papers, "Hey Babe."

"Hello?"

Rolling his eyes, Dunlop is visibly annoyed that his companion of two decades either cannot hear him, or is for whatever reason, pretending to not recognize his voice.

"Can you hear me?" Ellen pleads.

"Yes, Dear."

"Am I on speaker?" Ellen asks.

Shaking his head, Dunlop looks off into the distance, and then closes his eyes to assist in a quick, impromptu meditation session before answering, "Yes, Dear."

"Where are you?"

Exhaling deeply, Dunlop purposely composes himself and fakes an air of carefree, "Driving."

"Where?"

No longer able to pretend to be someone else, going someplace else, Dunlop's voice begins to move to monotone, "I have a meeting, and then I'll be home."

"With who?"

Shaking his head at the phone on the passenger seat, Dunlop sneers, "An associate."

"Who?"

Closing his eyes once again, Dunlop answers her innocent question as if it was meant to be rhetorical, since he feels like he's answered this same question a thousand times over the past six months, "You don't know him."

"Is this for work?"

Running on fumes and in bad need of a spiritual tune-up, Dunlop begins to add an edge to his voice, "That's what associates are for. If it was for pleasure, I'd be meeting a friend."

"And if it was to get laid, you'd be meeting a whore!"

Smirking, while shaking his head to a conversation that had run its course long ago, Dunlop can't help but mock her misguided misgivings, "But we both know I can't afford whores, honey."

"A guy from the bank called today."

Dunlop's eyes go wide, as his face grows pale, "What did you tell him?!"

"I told him what you told me to tell him!"

Now frantic, Dunlop punches the steering wheel, then slams the center console, "Why did you pick up the phone?!?!"

"They used a local number."

A look of absolute incredulity sweeps his face, and Dunlop is speechless for a moment as he searches for a rebuttal, "So?!?!"

"They always use 800 numbers. Do we owe someone else now?"

Staring back out the window, to once again concentrate on driving, Dunlop exhales just slightly, "No, it's a VOIP trick."

"Who's the VOIP? Another agency? Is it criminal?"

Squinting at the phone in disbelief, Dunlop realizes just how naive his wife is, "No. Nothing... They use local numbers via the Internet."

"How was I supposed to know they'd do that?"

Once again closing his eyes and slowly shaking his head, Dunlop is frustrated and fatigued, "You wouldn't, that's why they do it. It's a trick. They tricked you... Look, I told you not to pick up the phone unless you knew the number."

"We have two kids on play dates! What if one of the calls is a parent? I can't pick up because we're... what? What's happening with the loan anyway?"

Raising a hand, as if Ellen was in the car, Dunlop tries to reassure her on an old story, that gets staler by the second, "It's fine. I got it. We're good."

"That's what you said last month, and the month before that."

Muscles noticeably tense in Dunlop's jaw, while spots of salmon surface on his china white skin, "I'm working on it. Alright?"

"You've been working on it for two years!"

Putting his hand through his greasy, long, unkempt hair, Dunlop deflates in his seat, lowering his voice to reflect his new posture, "It's the home stretch... Bear with me."

"I got another letter today."

Dunlop glares at the phone, clenching his fist, "Don't open it!"

"It came certified. I had to sign for it."

Shaking his head quickly, Dunlop furiously scans the intersection, while parked at a red light, "Just don't open it."

"It's from a law firm."

Checking his rearview mirror for someone who's not there, Dunlop screams his command, "Just don't open it!"

"A man came to the house on Saturday? Sherman said a man came to the door and gave you some papers?"

Dunlop pauses as he scans the passenger seat for an answer, before taking back control of the wheel and his voice, "Yeah…"

"Were you served papers? From who?"

Desperately trying to remain cool while sweating bullets, Dunlop tries to unsuccessfully temper his wife's fears with fluff, "It's just bank protocol."

"For what?"

Dunlop does a once-over of both side view mirrors, then readjusts his rearview mirror, before exhaling, "I got to go."

"Where?"

A now red faced Dunlop wails white hot anger, "I already told you! I'm going to meet an associate!"

"Why?"

Desperately trying to claw back control of his anger, Dunlop slowly states, "For business…"

"I can't take this anymore!"

Seemingly lost in thought, Dunlop exhales and gently caresses the phone, as if it was his wife's cheek, "I don't blame you…"

"Someone came by today…"

Dunlop springs from his slouched position, ramming his hands into the steering wheel from locked arms, as if he's being hit by another car, instead of yet another piece of bad news. With every muscle in his arched back tense, and white knuckles at the ten and two position, Dunlop braces for impact as he frantically fires out, "Who? You didn't answer the door? I told you under no circumstances do you answer the fucking door!!!!"

"I didn't. And don't yell at me! I didn't even see him… OK!"

Dunlop searches the car in shock, looking for her answer to make sense somewhere, "How do you know someone came by if you didn't see them? What did they leave?"

"Nothing. Marge saw a man looking around our house when I was at the store. She said he looked around the property and left."

Dunlop spits, "Nosy bitch!"

"She cares about us! And she wasn't snooping. He was standing on our front lawn for Christ's sake! You're lucky she didn't call the cops!"

Rolling his eyes again in complete disgust, Dunlop has lost all patience for his wife and life, but tries desperately to hold them both for as long as he can. "He was with the bank. It's called a drive-by. Most likely wanted to get an idea of value."

"Why would he need that? Are we losing the house?!"

"No! I told you—banks are all about procedures. We're fine."

"Marge said he didn't look like a business man. Looked real big and mean. Are you in trouble?"

His wife's last statement gives Dunlop pause. Before he answers her with far more control than he has since word one of their broken record of a phone call, Dunlop peers into his rearview mirror, "I'm fine."

"Do I need to leave and go to my mother's? What's happening? Are you meeting this man now?"

"No."

"You know who this man is?"

Dunlop's voice raises slightly, partially revealing the ruse, "I didn't say that. I said I wasn't meeting him."

"How would you know that if you don't know who he is?"

Fluttering his eyes as he exhales, "Because the man I'm meeting has no idea who I am, nor why we're meeting."

"That doesn't sound very Kosher."

With a quick, cynical smirk, Dunlop regretfully remembers something he's said before, while saying goodbye to his wife forever, "Kosher... I got to go."

"Will you be home for dinner?"

A distracted Dunlop drones, "No..."

"When then?"

"Don't wait up. I got to make a couple of stops."

"What if I need you to pick up one of the boys later?"

"Leave a message."

"Your mailbox is full."

"I'll empty it now." With that said, Dunlop abruptly hangs up the phone before his wife can offer more dialogue to a conversation that was over before it had begun.

Scanning his phone, he notices two things that instantly infuriate him. One, he doesn't have much of a charge left, and two, he has ten messages! Shaking his head, while grinding his teeth, he squeezes the phone, as if he's trying to juice it. Biting the bullet, he thumbs the open envelope button to check his messages.

**Message 1**: This is Mr. Rodgers from Credit Care, we're – Dunlop presses erase.

**Message 2:** (Automated voice) Please call Bank United customer care at – Dunlop presses erase.

**Message 3:** Mr. Dunlop, this is Michael at Michael's Auto Repair. I need – Dunlop presses erase, closes his eyes briefly, and utters a faint, "Fuck".

**Message 4:** (Automated voice) This is an attempt to collect a debt, any information – Dunlop presses erase.

**Message 5:** Professor Dunlop… It's Dean Frazier. I need to speak with you first thing in the morning… before you step foot in your classroom. If you call my office before the morning, leave a detailed message as to when you plan on coming in. Dunlop presses erase with more force than is needed. Staring with red-rimmed retinas at the phone, a bewildered Dunlop drops a dumbfounded, "What the fuck???" before resuming his message retrieval.

**Message 6:** In a thick Bronx accent, a man with little patience and education, tries his best to leave a cordial message, most likely due to the fact that it's recorded, "I'm getting tired of leaving messages, Dunlop. You know we need to talk, so let's keep this civilized between gentlemen. You have my number and other things that belong to me. I would appreciate you returning my call and my belongings, before it's too late to return them."

Dunlop hangs up the phone as he cringes, almost to the point of shuddering.

His car stutters as if it shares his sentiment, and when he scans the dash for the guilty gauge, he sees an empty tank of gas is his downfall. "Shit!" Dunlop immediately darts a glance in every direction for a gas station, his panicked state hindering his ability to recollect where the closest station should be. While he's frantically spinning his head on a swivel and veering in and out of slow-moving traffic, the phone rings again. Dunlop snatches the phone, bringing it close enough to his face so that he can look at the caller ID and the road at the same time. It's Tommy—the same man who had left the last message.

"Shit!" Dunlop throws the phone against the passenger side door where it drops out of sight, somewhere between the doorsill and seat. "Shit!"

Searching for a station in vain, muttering inaudible curses, he yanks on his hair with his right, while strangling the steering wheel with his left. Discovering eureka across the intersection of a red light, Dunlop let's out a guttural, "Fuck yeah!" The car begins to sputter and then buck, signaling the last shot-glass of petrol. He tenses his hands around the wheel, for he knows he has one shot at getting diagonally across the intersection. If he stops, he stops for good; therefore he's got to time the light just right, for the oncoming traffic won't yield to him regardless of the insults he hurls at them.

Furthermore, rush-hour is taking shape, and once the intersection fills up, he'll be in the death throes of gridlock, with thousands of angry commuters behind him demanding that he go straight instead of left. He panics, and blows the red light, almost getting walloped from the side by a car looking to make the yellow. Cursing himself for not seeing the oncoming traffic, as well as not looking for a traffic cop prior to gunning the gap, he dreads the impending drive-by dress-down from the crazed commuter, "You stupid fucking cock-sucking fuck bag, I'll kick your fucking throat in!" Luckily for Dunlop, the man yells his hatred without ever slowing down, let alone stopping to follow through on his threat.

Slamming into the uneven parking lot of the gas station, Dunlop tries to make a beeline for the only open pump, but is beat to it by a large black man driving an air-conditioning Ford service van, coated in a thin layer of white spray paint, masking a gang war of graffiti. He knows that a physical altercation to decide the pump's pecking order will end poorly for him, so he beats his steering wheel in the only one-way fight he'd ever win. His tantrum is interrupted by the car stalling. "No! Fuck! Oh for fuck's sake!" Dunlop rests his head on the wheel for a moment, and then abruptly pushes back and slams it against the headrest. Closing his eyes from the pain and disgust, he lets out a deep exhale. Prying them open once again to check on availability, he's rewarded for his vigilance. Pump number four is twenty feet away and currently being vacated by a well-groomed business woman in a gray 5 Series, donning a donut-sized spare supporting the passenger front. He attempts to start the car again, hoping for a minimum of a mouse's piss puddle worth of petrol in the tank, but is rewarded with nothing more than the engine turning over. "Fuck!"

Knowing that churning the engine will result in a drained battery on top of a drained gas tank, Dunlop resigns himself to push power for the final stretch. Slamming the car into neutral, he violently pushes the door open wide, leaving himself plenty of room to hop out quickly. Once he's jettisoned from the vehicle, he establishes a foothold before he pushes the car up the slight embankment, by bracing himself against the door and straight-arming the steering wheel with his right. "Hey, can I get some help here?" Dunlop solicits no one in particular. Fully aware before uttering a word that no one will lift a pinky to help him, he begins to push the car on his own before the other patrons have a chance to pretend to do something important.

The twenty-foot slight incline leaves him physically spent by the time the car caps the crest. Adding injury to insult, Dunlop clips his leg as he races to jam himself into the seat, in hopes of applying the brake in time, as to not tap the bumper of the $95K, tri-coated pearl white, Cadillac Escalade, fueling up at the pump in front of his. Slamming to a stop mere millimeters from the large SUV, Dunlop mutters an exhausted, "Mother fucker…" Frantically fumbling through his pockets, Dunlop finally locates his bloated wallet, and kisses it hello.

His heartfelt reunion is cut short, as he yanks card after card from the credit coffin, tossing them to the passenger seat floor, after mentally reviewing the reason it's already been canceled, or overdrawn. With a sigh of relief, Dunlop unsheathes his Discover card, brandishing it triumphantly like Excalibur before his foe. With him since college, the card, like his car, doesn't tote the same panache it once did, but it still works every time he goes to use it, unlike everything else as of late, including his dick.

He squares off with the pump and sets his shoulders, taunting the card-reader by absently tapping his palm with the plastic. Without warning, he slams the card in the slot, like an interrogator slapping a silent suspect. Waiting for what seems like an eternity for the machine to spill the beans, it finally denies him with indifference. Shocked by its stance, Dunlop flips out, "What the fuck? This is good!" Looking around for someone to yell at, he zeroes in on the elderly Latino female gas attendant lounging behind a bullet-proof glass partition, and screams, "What the fuck?!?!? I got room on this card!"

A speaker above Dunlop's head crackles on and the smoke-scarred voice of the older woman delivers the bad news, "We don't take Discova."

"Fuck you!"

"Sorry sweetie, I only fuck AMEX owners."

Dunlop knows the argument is futile, and begins to scan his wallet for any form of currency that can be potentially converted to petrol. *Nothing!* He then embarks on a spastic search for loose change, but it's an egg hunt he's been on more than once this year, and expects he's already exhausted the resources of every crack, crevasse, fold, and oft-used pocket months ago. "Shit, shit, shit!"

Kneeling outside the driver's door, he's past caring for the condition of his clothes. Upon a final inspection, a defeated Dunlop rests his sweaty brow on the cracked and faded cushion. Knowing his prayers will go unanswered, by a God he's never truly believed in, he lifts his head and blows out the remains of his breath. Clinging to the car door, he uses it as a makeshift crutch, managing to stand without placing weight on the injured leg. Once erect, he cradles his head with both hands, and spins around in a hapless 360, while staggering on wobbly legs. He's on the verge of exploding into a full-frontal panic attack, when a moment of absolute clarity alleviates his anxieties. Grabbing his bag out of the trunk, he simply walks from the car, like he's leaving a rental at the airport in a no parking zone, because he's late for an important flight.

The speaker crackles on and the lady is obviously perturbed by the unforeseen events, "Hey, what the Hell, Pal?"

Dunlop doesn't answer, for he's left the car, just like he's left his wife – high and dry. As he walks away with a noticeable limp, which he'd received from positioning his car, people stand about, gawking at him incredulously. He doesn't hear their condescending comments, nor his own cellphone ringing in the car, which has Tommy's name on the Caller ID…

# Chapter 2

# Dressing on the Side

Shilly's was your classic Arthur Avenue restaurant establishment. The front of the two-story building was a faded, beige stucco that was accented by pseudo-brick to give the aura of old. The windows, though classy in their own right, were marred by black iron security bars that had been painted far too many times to cover the rust, alerting any motivated cat burglar that they were most likely clinging to the side of the building by a couple of rusty screws, rather than securing it.

But, if you were a local criminal, you'd know better than to test the building's defenses in the first place. Matter of fact, if the front and back doors were both left wide open in the middle of the night with a duffle bag full of hundreds plopped on the kitchen's chopping block, with a hot meal by its side awaiting the brazen burglar, the meal and money would still be there in the morning without a bite, or Benjamin, taken. The reason was risk versus reward. The reward was simple enough, a full belly and bank account. But as appetizing as that sounded, the risk was just far too high that the owner of the establishment would find out it was you who stole what was his. His name couldn't be found on the county court land deed to the building, but everyone for ten city blocks knew he owned the building, lock, stock, and barrel, along with the men who silently patrolled it.

The classic Italian restaurant that snugly seated seventy-five people on a Thursday night, served that very man upstairs in a palatial parlor more evenings than not. Eliseo Franklin

Catanzano, aka "Ellie Meat Hooks", was one of the most ferocious men to ever walk Arthur Ave. His famous quote, "*Why I'm gonna do this is business. How I'm gonna do it is personal,*" was urban legend.

Ellie, as close friends and family referred to him, had rapidly risen in the ranks of the Cantanzano crime family by offing his twin brother as punishment for ratting out their uncle when they were both busted for illegally transporting cigarettes from South Carolina some twenty-five years prior. Everyone knew then that Ellie meant business, for he not only decapitated his twin with a meat cleaver right in front of a dozen employees of the Hunts Point Market, but he picked up the headless corpse, and tossed it onto a meat hook, leaving him to hang for his co-workers and competing families to see.

If the brutal slaying wasn't bone-chilling enough for the traumatized audience, what Ellie said next sealed the deal for the title of **Baddest Ass Motherfucker in all the Bronx**. "Age him for the day, then sell him to the gooks in the morning, cause if they're gonna use rats in their beef and broccoli, it might as well be my brother."

Everyone knew right then and there that Ellie meant business. They also knew his business model ran on three things: loyalty, brutal punishment for betraying said loyalty, and thirdly, no one was above one and two. That level of commitment and accountability commanded immediate respect and power throughout the Bronx. No one questioned his commitment to the Family after that day. No one…

Emblazoned by his new-found notoriety within the Family, Eliseo solidified his ascension to the position of "Don" by taking one bold move after another. Instead of losing himself in the Family's criminal activities like his siblings and cousins, which ranged from extortion to smuggling, Ellie focused on growing the face of the franchise—Arthur Ave's burgeoning fresh food market and restaurant scene. He consolidated the Arthur Ave food businesses like an investment banker would roll-up car dealerships in the Midwest, making the Family's money-laundering companies into legitimate high-end food servicers and importers, with clientele from Boca Raton to Kennebunkport. Within five years he could make anyone for ten city blocks kiss his ring. Within ten, the first politician openly smooched it on the steps of Our Lady of Mount Carmel Church after a beautiful spring Sunday Mass.

+ + +

Two doors past the well-appointed bathrooms, an old narrow and rickety staircase with one sharp turn leads to a 12' x 12' waiting room, draped in ornate burgundy and gold-weave patterned wallpaper and imported antique furniture. The tastefully executed, timepiece of Italian Renaissance, is occupied by two large men in finely-tailored business suits, lounging about, preoccupied with their newspapers and cuticles. Of course, the cavalier couch potato persona is a farce, for the two are actually highly-trained sentries, donning high-tech body armor, made from spider silk and Kevlar beneath their suits. In addition to the latest in ballistic grade body shells, both men also conceal dual nickel-plated Uzi's, with twenty extra magazines integrated into the vests of their three-piece suits, to act as an additional layer of ballistic grade protection in case they receive fire before they can give it.

At the opposite side of the room stands a large, thick, ornate door, sourced from an illegally cut Sequoia tree from Northern California. The door, an antique in its own right, is large and expensive enough to adorn any mansion along the Gold Coast. The door's size of four-feet wide and nine-feet high, made it impossible to bring it up the stairs. Luckily for Ellie, he owned Arthur Building Company, dba ABC Construction, a commercial construction company, that had a high-rise crane in its inventory. The joke in the local precinct and FBI office, was ABC actually stood for Arthur Burial Company, because the foundations poured by the company had more bodies than sand in the mix.

Being the door was higher than the original eight-foot ceiling, meant Ellie had to raise the roof once the massive door was positioned. Having to raise an entire roof to accommodate a single door, left Ellie the butt of jokes across the various branches of law enforcement. Surveillance teams for both the FBI and local law enforcement joked daily on how much time and money Ellie was wasting, building the rooms around the door. When he screamed at his construction crew, demanding that they do this or that, in order to accommodate the massive door, agents would turn down the sound on the boom mics and dub their own demands, mocking Ellie's ostentatious audacity. The building's age and infrastructure, meant Ellie had to spend considerable money on reinforcing the bones of the building, turning a mundane styling statement into a multi-million-dollar renovation.

The jokes about Ellie's lavish spending died quicker than a rat in his organization when the truth of the construction finally hit home. Ellie had used the door as a ruse to completely change the inside of the building. Sure, the walls were now ten-feet high, but now they were also one-foot thick, with an additional two inches of lead plate insulation. The ceiling was also reinforced with metal and concrete, as was the floor. The downstairs looked to be updated as well, which is standard fare for any restaurant every decade or so, but behind the faux brick that was adorned by hand painted murals of Venice and Rome, were now walls comprised of both nine inches of reinforced cement and three inches of ballistic grade steel. In addition to the massive infrastructure upgrade, the basement was said to now have hidden tunnels to several basements of nearby buildings, affording Ellie's men unfettered and unchecked access to his new headquarters, which couldn't be monitored by any of the latest and greatest surveillance equipment. And being that Ellie also ran all the local Unions that had anything to do with the municipalities, the agencies couldn't even get an agent posing as a "Cable Guy" onto an adjoining pole to tap the wires.

What's more? In a last-ditch effort to thwart Ellie's new impenetrable compound, the FBI worked with the local building code violation bureau in hopes they could have Ellie's building razed, due to the fact that it wasn't built to code, only to find out Ellie had already predicted that bush-league move, and not only paid off the inspectors and local zoning boards, but had his plans secretly approved a year prior to construction and grandfathered in. The bottom line was, no bullets, radio waves, laser beams, listening devices, or cameras could assist the law in Ellie's plans, and department heads rolled once the news hit the big desks, faster than they rolled in Ellie's organization when someone screwed the pooch.

Ellie's new digs already had several new nicknames bestowed upon it by law enforcement, the competing Families, his own Family, and even local shop keepers who knew the inside scoop. The one that was gaining the most traction was The Tomb, because Ellie rarely dove into the day to day minutia any longer unless he had to dial up some death, thus if you were going to see Ellie from the outside, you were never going to see the outside again...

Sitting behind his handcrafted, Italian Rosewood desk, Ellie was an imposing figure. Once a muscular man, Ellie was now the victim of his own success, spending his millions equally among his toys, women, and food. Years of gorging and ordering others to run around to do his bidding gave Ellie a deep breath that sounded as if he needed the assistance of an inhaler. Though Ellie's chances of coming in second in a two-man race were slim to none, the years of working the meat racks and shipping containers at Hunts Point gave him the massive forearms, legs, and back of a silverback gorilla. The multiple scars running down each of his cheeks, due to the unsafe working environment of mid-century food services and of course, Mob services, resulted in a nose broken so many times, Humpty Dumpty's men would have winced and walked from the job. If Ellie's body was a boat, it would have been an Alaskan tugboat—big, brawny, beaten, and battered, with way too much salt and cold drinks comprising its diet.

In complete contrast to Ellie's body, were the suits that Ellie used to hide it. Woven by hand from the finest silks Italy and the Orient could offer, they were tailored by his own in-house artisan, who also cobbled his custom-designed shoes. His personal, on premise barber, meticulously trimmed Ellie's head no less than three times a week, while keeping his multi-chin hairless with two open razor shaves a day. Refusing to accept a five o'clock shadow, even though he made his living in shadows, was one of the many ironies that comprised the criminal mastermind, known as Ellie Meat Hooks. To that end, his weekly manicures and pedicures were from the same Asian girls he transported into the City via Hunts Point shipping containers for his human trafficking ring.

Though his clothing and oral hygiene were impeccable, his eating etiquette, mannerisms, and all around social grace were anything but. In the end, Ellie was a thug's thug, and no matter how many layers of lipstick were slapped on the pig, he was still happiest rolling around in his own shit.

"I'm done with this fuck's bullshit!" Ellie barks to no one in particular.

A massive muscle draped in finely fitted silks, offers a sinister smile along with his unquestioning. "Say the word, Boss," the killer casually comments, while cracking his knuckles.

+ + +

Carl "Yessie" Cassese was a bully's bully. In his illustrious career, he had muscled, extorted, and, yes, disposed of more people than he cared to remember, all for the chance to one day be right where he was—with his hands resting on his boulder-sized beer belly, four and half-feet off to the right of the most powerful man in the Bronx.

Raised in a house three blocks from Arthur Avenue in a low rent apartment, Carl's dad was mid-level management for a Family on the decline. Shortly before his father was found with no arms in the woods of Pelham Park with a ball of fresh mozzarella lodged in his mouth, he'd bestowed upon Carl some much needed career advice. His father was adamant that being a henchman, lieutenant, soldier, or any other job for that matter, within the Mob that had him on the streets, carrying out the orders from those within the inner sanctum, was a job that would one day see him brutally murdered more likely than not.

That if he was going to be stupid enough to stay in the Bronx and follow in his father's footsteps, he should specialize in security for someone who was powerful and paranoid. His father's reasoning was simple: if you get shot while guarding the Family's head of the household, your family tree is about to be chopped down anyway, making you a dead man walking. Therefore, you might as well go out in style, being mowed down in the most exclusive restaurant in town, rather than gutted like a pig in the alley behind it.

"Carl, you're not smart, but you're not a complete schmuck. Matter of fact you're half as dumb as my dumbest, Mikey, but you see, he's a fucking retard, so that makes you somewhere near stupid, which is still better than an idiot on most days."

"Yes Papa."

"Your brother Johnny, on the other hand, is a fucking idiot, and he'll be a burden on the Family until he's dead, because he's so fucking dumb, he doesn't even know he's an idiot. You'll have to help Mama with him."

"Yes Papa."

"Not only are you smarter than your brothers, you're smart enough to know, you're not smart enough to get out of trouble, but yet, you're smart enough to know how to stay out of trouble… and that's good."

"Yes Papa."

"You're also a natural 'Yes Man', which is good if your job is to say yes."

"Yes Papa."

"I'm sending you to Kenny's Corner on 5th Street. They'll teach you to box there and make sure people say yes to your questions, so people know not to question you. Whatever they don't teach you there, I'll tutor you when you're old enough to keep your eyes open and your mouth shut."

"Yes Papa."

"Remember Carl, you find who's rising to the top, catch their coattails, and stay off the streets until you retire. Retire early. Complain of lower back pain and foot issues. Start forgetting things you remember that will annoy people, but won't piss them off. Whatever you do, don't retire to Florida. Go somewhere that's more than a direct flight away. Open a pizza parlor outside of New York and people will line up to give you money, that ya otherwise gotta fight for here."

"Yes Papa."

"And Remember Carl, don't make enemies unless you have to, especially within the Family. If you've got to knock someone out, never hit 'em while they're down. And when they're down, be a gracious victor by helping them get up, unless you're planning on ending them. If that's the case, don't stop punching until you see bone through blood."

"Yes Papa."

Looking at Tommy, Carl wants to knock him out, but doesn't feel the urge to keep punching, so he unclenches his fists. He also knows he doesn't want to fill Tommy's shoes if he were no longer wearing them, so he refrains from dressing him down.

Facing Tommy, Ellie performs a deep tissue massage on his temples, as he rests his eyes closed, "Tommy, did you know this fuck, Dunlop could lose his fucking house in a foreclosure?"

"No Ellie. I swear. I thought he was on the up and up," Tommy bellows with great sincerity.

Tommy is a short, stocky Italian, with olive skin, blonde hair, and sky blue eyes. In addition to his aesthetically pleasing attributes, the muscled Mediterranean Ken doll has a movie star smile that rests upon a chiseled chin that would emasculate The Fantastic Four's, The Thing. Though throughout the years he could have said and done what he willed with the women, Tommy was a gentlemen's gentleman, and lived and died by the codes of honor that his father taught him so many years ago, on the unforgiving streets of the lower Bronx.

Naturally good natured, Tommy was the last person you'd expect the Boss to send when delivering the final collection notice.

But even though Tommy was an indispensable asset to the Family, and someone who was truly revered within the Family, he wasn't safe from Ellie's wrath. "On the up and up? He's leveraging his entire fucking life via a vicious loan shark, and you think he's on the up and up? Are you fucking retarded?" a flabbergasted Ellie admonishes.

The even larger and less shapely stooge to Ellie's left, nicknamed "The Lake", barks a laugh, straining the top button of his too-tight tailored dress shirt.

Tommy glares at The Lake, before pleading his case, "No Ellie. I swear."

Looking to the other guys in the room with his arms out, Ellie offers some rhetorical, "You swear? You swear you didn't know he was leveraged to the hilt, or you swear you're not retarded?"

The Lake giggles like a chimp before going back to eating a cuticle on a hand that looks to have been mauled by a shark.

Tommy clears his throat and sets his jacket before answering, "I swear I thought he was down on his luck, Ellie. But as Christ as my witness, I believed in my heart that he was a pretty conservative guy. Nice family, nice job… And to be honest with you Ellie, real estate ain't my thing."

Ellie seems taken back by Tommy's honesty, sincerity, and revelation that he isn't well versed in certain financial markets, as he carefully repositions himself further back in his chair. "Oh, real estate ain't your thing? You have a thing? You're an expert in something else?"

"Ellie…," cautions Angie. Ellie's right hand man and Underboss since he became The Don, Angie was as level headed as Ellie was erratic. They made a dynamic duo of sorts, with Angie being more than just a confidant of Ellie's, but Ellie's best, and possibly only real friend.

Waving Angie off with a raised finger, Ellie refocuses on Tommy, "In what?!"

"I'm not an expert in anything Ellie," Tommy offers.

"Wrong again! You're an expert in fucking up!" Ellie screams.

The Lake cackles again, but this time louder, caring less for those who overhear.

"I'm sorry Ellie… I'll make you whole. I swear on my mother's grave…" Tommy offers with great sincerity.

"Oh yeah? How much is Mr. Dumbfuck into us for?" inquires Ellie, turning to his tubby Underboss, Angie.

Angie gives it his best Rain Man, as he twiddles his stubby fingers on an invisible calculator, "With interest… five hundred large. Add penalties and interest on penalties, various late fees and so forth… Figure an additional 200."

Taking an exaggerated double take of Angie's arithmetic, Ellie apparently adds some additional hidden costs to his final tally, "This fucking piker owes me a million dollars and you're planning on making me whole!?"

"You bet Ellie," Tommy willingly replies all too quickly for anyone's liking, including his own.

Angie illuminates the pertinent information, before Ellie can cast further darkness upon the day, "Our Professor is supposedly making one last attempt at a deal today."

Ellie slams one of his huge hams on his desk, "This cocksucker is spending more of my fucking money?!"

Tommy literally jumps to address the misunderstanding, shooting his arms straight forward with palms fully exposed, as if he's trying to put the brakes on Ellie's runaway imagination, "No way Ellie! This is money he's already spent. He's just waiting for it to come in."

"Where?" Ellie quickly questions.

Angie interrupts Tommy, "Hunts Point Market. Coming in on some food shipment out of Central America."

Looking from Tommy to Angie, Ellie makes his joke of the week, "What the fuck is it? A golden banana?"

Tommy doesn't see the humor, "Something really, really rare and expensive."

"It fucking better be!" Ellie roars.

Angie, who had twice the fat as Ellie, on half the frame, rubs his chins as he recalls the deal, "It's supposedly some kind of scepter, or sword."

Miffed, Ellie looks for clarification, "A scepta?"

Angie quickly adds, "He thinks it's covered in gold and rare jewels."

Immediately enraged, "I don't care if it's covered in the shit from the wetback's asshole it was smuggled in with—how much?"

Angie offers his amateur appraisal, "If the description's accurate… The gold alone will make you whole. A couple of times over…"

Ellie takes immediate stock of the potential upside of a deal gone south a winter ago, "Gold, huh... You think he's bullshitting?"

"I think he's telling the truth, Ellie," The Lake surmises.

+ + +

Perry Tobanomo, aka The Lake, was on his third nickname, largely due to his love of food and music. At the age of seven, a portly Perry was nicknamed Ferry the Homo, a play on words for Perry Como, by a bully in school, because he loved to sing Golden Oldies at lunch recess. His love of theater and dance solidified his nickname until it changed after he bludgeoned another Wise Guy to death from a competing Family with a candelabra at a wedding of a mutual neighborhood friend, after said Wise Guy heckled him while he belted *New York, New York* with the band at the bride and groom's request.

By the time the wedding had unceremoniously ended, Perry Tobanomo went from Ferry the Homo, to Perry Como, which would serve him well in the next stage of his life as inmate, singing for cigarettes instead of being sold for them. Perry, who went straight from a fancy suit with cuffs, to handcuffs and a jumpsuit, was privately relieved, for he'd rather be one man's bitch when the lights went out, instead of everyone's bitch while the lights were still on.

Upon his early release for good behavior, Perry had both doubled in size and lost his love of singing soprano, and thus his nickname went from Perry Como, to Lake Como. His promotion to Wise Guy came almost as fast as his new nickname, largely due to the fact that Ellie had recently declared war on the very Family that hosted the wedding where The Lake had answered his critics. Making a statement by elevating an undeserving Perry to Wise Guy had taken everyone by surprise, including The Lake himself. Dispelling any doubt that The Lake's promotion had zero to do with any form of merit or goodwill, versus a vicious message to a warring Family, was Ellie's complete disdain and distrust of The Lake's input or advice.

+ + +

"You think like I shit. Twice a week and it's a mess!"

Lenny Long Legs, who thinks even less of Perry than Ellie does, lets out a hearty chuckle at Ellie's appraisal.

Angie, which was short for Angelo Antorino, follows up like a true professional, refusing to acknowledge the banter, while bringing the conversation back to constructive. "The Professor believed whatever he told me, while Ramon and Mikey were working out the kinks in his neck. Whether that's true…" Angie finishes with a shrug and a lifted lip to suggest anything was possible.

Ellie raises an impatient hand to Angie without looking his way, "Either way, I'm done with Mr. Dunlop. I wanna cash in our loan, his ass, and whateva assets he hasn't already pilfered."

"You got it Ellie," Angie answers.

Directing his gaze to Tommy, Ellie asks, "Did you get the fuck to sign over his life insurance policy like I told you?"

"We couldn't," Tommy reluctantly replies.

"Why?" Ellie interrogates.

"Some stipulations… red tape… etcetera…" Tommy timidly answers.

Squinting his eyes in disgust, "Excedra?"

Tommy takes note, "It was really complicated... Whole-life policies are like that, Ellie."

Ellie is clearly at his wit's end, "Who buys a fucking whole-life policy these days? What a schmuck. We lent money to a schmuck! A fucking schmuck!" Slamming both hams to the desk, Ellie is irate.

"I'm sorry Ellie," Tommy pleads.

Raising a finger, "I want him dead by dawn."

Tommy eagerly takes the assignment, "You got it Ellie. I'll take care of it personally."

But Ellie will have none of it. "No, you won't. You've fucked up enough today. Besides, you're too nice."

Hurt, Tommy argues an appeal, "I can do this Ellie."

Breathing through his mouth before he gives his final judgement, Ellie's tone comes down a notch. "I'm sure you could Tommy... I'm sure you could. But you see... I don't want to just do him, I want to do him right. And there's only one guy who can express my displeasure in Mr. Dunlop's dishonesty and incompetency."

Angie sensing where Ellie's rant is going, tries to signal the need for Ellie to pump the brakes on the crazy train before it jumps the tracks, "Ellie—"

But Ellie slams his foot down on the wrong pedal, and begins to bloviate, balls to the wall, "That's right! That's Goddamned fucking right, Baby!"

Tommy, as are the others, is clearly taken aback by the de facto choice, "Jeez Ellie. I hate you risking things with him..."

Now it's Ellie's chance to be taken aback, "Risking things? You give away a million of my hard-earned fucking dollars to a mummy-fucking book worm, on the verge of personal financial fucking ruin, to gamble on hidden fucking treasures from around the fucking globe, and now you want me to play it safe?"

Angie looks to steady the ship with some diplomacy, "Tommy meant no disrespect Ellie. It's just—"

"It's just what?" Ellie snaps. Looking to everyone in the room, one by one, then to no one in particular, "I need results, Gentlemen. I need to send a message—a clear and concise message."

Noticeably agitated, Tommy fidgets with his hands, as he continues to concentrate on the floor, in hopes of keeping grounded as he speaks out of turn. "The Razor's a loose cannon. That's all...", Tommy softly and sincerely stipulates.

Ellie blows off Tommy's statement for hyperbole, "Overzealous, yes. Loose cannon, no. He's got his shit together. Which is more than I can say for any of you fucks as of late!"

"He's had some issues following direction," Angie annotates.

Rolling his eyes, Ellie dismisses the discourse, "Is that it? He don't play well with others?"

"I'm referring to the attention he's brought upon the Family with some of the jobs as of late," Angie answers back with as much diplomacy as he can muster.

But Ellie holds his ground and emphatically backs his nomination "Since when did the Cantanzano Family shy away from some free PR?"

Taking a big step to Ellie's desk, Angie extends a soft hand to Ellie's shoulder, "He enjoys his work a little too much for some of the guy's liking, that's all."

Ellie gently swats Angie's hand away from his shoulder showing his annoyance, but also his love and respect, "He's an artist, Angie—a Renaissance man if you will… Besides, like I tell my kids, do what you love for a living and you'll never work another day in your life."

"You got that right, Boss," Perry pontificates.

"Stab yourself," Ellie snaps.

"Sorry, Boss," Perry sniffles.

Lenny laughs once again at Perry's expense, this time noticeably louder. In Lenny's defense, it had taken him twenty years of kissing, kicking, and working his ass off to earn his rank, versus Perry, who'd just sat on it for ten.

"What about the package?" Angie asks Ellie.

Leaning back in his massive, hand-stitched, coffee colored, Italian leather chair, "What about it?" Ellie replies. "As far as I'm concerned, that's another reason to send The Razor. I trust him implicitly. He's honest and capable. The exact mirror fucking opposite of our Mr. Dunlop."

"With all due respect, Ellie, he's a psychopath," Tommy quips quickly.

Through with the doubters and dissension, Ellie leans forward, raising his voice one octave below a yell. "I don't care about The Razor's mental state, his status in the community, his peer review ratings, nor the attention he garners this Family! What I care about is you making damn fucking sure he gets to the fucking market and gets my fucking treasure and Mr. Dunlop's balls!"

Quickly acquiescing to Ellie's rank and reasoning, Tommy reassures Ellie, "I'll get him on the horn right now."

"No you won't. You'll go and pick The Razor up, and personally escort him to the job. And remember Tommy… I want Dunlop's balls."

"You got it Ellie. Balls and all."

Pointing a finger at Tommy, "Make sure you do Tommy. Make sure you bring back my treasure and the Professor's balls on a roll, with sweet peppers, provolone and broccoli rabe."

"You got it Ellie."

"And as always Tommy—dressing on the side."

"You got it Ellie. Dressing on the side…"

# Chapter 3

## Close Quarters

Some say having to shoot a perp is the greatest test a cop can face during his career. Pulling the gun from its holster and making the conscious decision to take a human life is profound and everlasting. Those who have taken a life will tell you over a drink at a social occasion how it has altered their existence, and that there's not a day that goes by that they don't think of the person they've killed, or the loved ones that have been left behind in the physical realm, while the deceased takes off on their final journey into the beyond.

If the guy they killed had kids, the officer will be able to tell you their names and ages, and in some cases, will even keep tabs on them from afar throughout their lives. He'll tell you if they're in college, or if they have kids of their own, even what their names are. Some cops even befriend the family and assist in raising the kids, at a minimum sending gifts and/or money—especially around the holidays when the guilt is most powerful.

Though the thoughts are admirable and many officers find themselves on the sucker's side of a glory hole trying to forget their troubles, the truth of what an officer dreads the most only surfaces once an officer has had several drinks throughout the night, and the tight tail has already left the party with other shlongs, and thus, there's no one left to impress with bullshit, sob stories. That's when the stark reality of the day-to-day grind of a professional's career comes to rear its ugly head, and the officer professes what really frightens him.

You see, the reality is, an officer doesn't fear shooting a piece of shit, and taking said shit off the streets for good. In fact, he wakes up every morning, hoping to have a legitimate reason to kill a drug dealer, pimp, or chester. Taking a low life's life is something officers dream of, but sadly, fewer officers are able to achieve that badge of honor per year, than professional football players achieve the pinnacle of their career, a Super Bowl ring. And though there are only 1,664 humans on thirty-two teams vying for the fifty-two rings awarded players in the NFL each year, there are over 1.5 million good guys, between the FBI, ATF, Border Patrol and various Sheriff departments, as well as federal, state, county and local city police, who dream of that elusive shot at the title.

If slaying a scumbag is the Super Bowl, a stakeout is spring training for the bush league. To some officers, the recurring nightmare of a long, protracted stakeout, based on faulty data and stale leads, is a prison sentence. That's right—sitting in a hot, stinking car, or blacked-out van for hours on end is Hell on Earth. Sitting in said vehicle with someone who grates on your nerves like nails on a chalkboard, makes Hell go from hot, to humid. The gridlock at the intersection of Pain and Misery continues well past rush hour and into the night for many embattled partnerships, and the dream team of Vassy and Putin was as cliché as a hand-rolled cigarette, being lit by a matchstick in a spaghetti western.

Petro Romulus Petadirica, aka Putin, was your classic sloppy Slavic. At six-foot six inches tall, Putin could have added another twenty pounds to his big-boned frame and still looked too thin. His thick and wavy shoulder-length, brown hair adorned the sides of a jawline that belonged on a Cro-Magnon skeleton in the Museum of Natural History. His face's saving grace was its deep-set green eyes, which made his otherwise poorly proportioned Neanderthal skull somewhat attractive in the right light. In his late thirties, Putin still had the acne and enthusiasm of a teenager, and could pass for a jock in his early twenties if he was needed for a sting operation. But unlike a lost "Generation Y'er", Putin knew his shortcomings, one of which was his fashion sense, or lack thereof. Caring less for his looks than a bridge troll, Putin compensated by willfully acquiescing to his wife's tastes, allowing her to not only buy his entire wardrobe, but pick out his daily attire, as well. Tolerating the dress-for-success mantra that assuaged his wife's fears that he wasn't finely focused on the corporate endgame of becoming the Chief of Police by the age of fifty, Putin would wait until he got to the sanctuary of the squad car before pulling his shirt out of his pants and loosening his tie, resembling a private school kid on the bus ride home. Though more comfortable out of dress code, Putin was never out of sorts. Sharper than his aloofness advertised, Putin was a natural detective, due to his desire to let people talk, while he pretended not to listen.

His partner, Vassy, a portly Puerto Rican, had less hair than an Asian concubine and the personal hygiene to rival the Emperor himself. Manicures and pedicures were done weekly, and his balding head was professionally shaven twice a week, as well as waxed once a month. The remainder of his body had never produced a single hair outside of his privates, and even that field was clipped close since its first crop.

A foot shorter than Putin, Vassy was about the same weight: 220 pounds. Well-dressed and accessorized with shoes and jewelry that were well above his pay grade, Vassy was classic flash. Ninety-eight cents of every dollar he took home could be seen somewhere on his person. Living well above his means and not being well-known for great integrity, made Vassy the butt of jokes and hearsay, as well as the center of more than one internal investigation throughout his lackluster career. Smart enough to cover his tracks well enough to either stop, or stall a dozen inquiries into his integrity, Vassy couldn't emerge from the scrum of detective rank for what seemed to be half his career.

Of course, he would never acknowledge the perception of his corruption, nor his atrophied arrest record, coupled with his poor team player persona as reasons for his stalled carcass of a career. On the contrary, Vassy was smart enough to know that framing an argument was the only way to win one, especially when you're dead wrong, and thus he embraced the role of the embattled, disgruntled, minority to its absolute extreme conclusion.

And since Vassy was trying to win back time from the Father himself, he'd have to be a card shark. The ace up his sleeve was the race card, which he wielded every time he needed to double down on yet another poor hand he'd dealt himself. His current hand had him partners with Putin, a man ten years his junior and already greenlighted for yet another promotion, which stirred an already volatile mix of personalities. Poor chemistry wasn't helped by a dead-end case on a day hotter than Hell, in a car that had been to Hell and back. To add fuel to the fire, Putin's poorly timed, off-the-cuff humor always seemed to miss its mark on Vassy, exasperating an already toxic situation.

Therefore, things blew up quickly when Putin took the large hero he was devouring with an open chew and smeared a dollop of mayo on his lips, before slipping the hero between Vassy's legs in order to pretend to blow it.

"Hey, what the fuck? You tripping?" Vassy reprimands.

With mayo-smeared cheeks that were full of food, Putin fires back, "We're undercover. I'm trying to assimilate."

"You're not in the West Village, you freak!" Vassy roars.

"In today's world, self-expression has no address," Putin pontificates, with a smug smile.

"You look like a fucking freak show!" Vassy screams.

"I look like a guy having fun, unlike you," Putin fires back.

"I don't fake fun on a double shift, and I never fake fag!" Vassy snaps back.

"You're not faking anything, which is why you look like a cop on a stakeout." Pointing with his half-eaten hero into the distance, "Those guys at the loading dock have scanned this car two dozen times since we rolled up."

Blowing their cover would add an inconsolable insult to a season-ending injury, and Vassy wasn't looking to be their team's scapegoat, "Because of me? You're the one drawing attention to this car by going to third base with a hoagie."

Vassy's statement sets the stage for more of Putin's nonsense, "A hoagie? This is no hoagie, Compadre."

Vassy rolls his eyes, "Here we go…"

Holding it with a gentle love reserved for a newborn baby at a christening, Putin begins his sermon, "This authentic, legendary, delicacy is from one of the premier Italian eateries in all of Hunts Point, including Arthur Ave, which by default, makes it one of the best –"

"What the fuck do you know about fine Italian dining, you crazy Russian bastard?"

Feigning shock, Putin points out, "I'm a quarter Italian."

"Bullshit!"

"No, I swear. Mother's side. Northern of course," Putin frenetically follows up.

Prodding more than protesting, Vassy plays puzzled, "Anyone ever tell you, you look Irish?"

Shrugging a 'yes', "All the time. How do you think I got this job in the first place?"

Vassy offers a tight smile, "They must have been beside themselves when they found out there was a Rusky in their midst."

Contemplating what their reactions must have been, Putin takes a second before openly opining, "We're more alike than you think."

"You and who? Aliens?" Vassy inquires incredulously.

"Irish," Putin answers absently as he engulfs another fistful of food.

"How so?" Vassy quickly questions, adding more genuine curiosity to his tone than he intends.

Counting on his fingers to remember a list he's recited more than once, Putin fires off the similarities, "We both consume lots of potatoes and booze, have fair skin—"

Interrupting with a light-hearted chuckle, "Is Ass White a Crayola color?"

A perturbed Putin pontificates with even more zeal, "And... (raising his finger and wagging it slightly to emphasize his point) more importantly, both races have survived thousands of years of oppression, only to come to this (pointing downward) God forsaken country to be treated like secondary citizens!"

Looking quite taken by his partner's diatribe, Vassy remarks, "I didn't know you were so fond of the Irish."

Tilting his head in acknowledgement, Putin sets the record straight, "Understand their inner demons? Yes. Sympathize with their hardship? Yes. Respect their contribution to this great country we live in? 100%. That said, I won't take shit from a Mick."

"Term of endearment right there, Papi."

Taking another massive bite from the hero, Putin garbles a passionate, "You know what I'm talking about..."

Squinting his eyes, Vassy inquires, "What does 'Mick' mean?"

Shrugging his shoulders, Putin responds with a cavalier, "No clue."

Dispatch comes over the speaker – "Bravo 1-9-55 we have gunfire reported on Arthur Ave, south of 181st Street."

Smiling, while wagging his hero, Putin coos glowingly of the night's freak forecast, "I can feel the tension today, like a hot, wet, fart dripping down my leg..."

"You got that right, Amigo, it stinks... Wait! What the fuck!?" Suddenly, aggressively sniffing the air with flaring nostrils, Vassy cringes from an apparent offensive odor that had been previously undetected. Physically traumatized, Vassy's eyes bug out, as his shoulders arch, and breath seemingly stops. Resembling a human who's fallen in a frozen pond, Vassy's bodily functions shut down as his neurological system attempts to process the atrocious aroma overload.

Still chewing like a Great White with a baby porpoise in its jaws, Putin shows little remorse, "Sorry, Bro. This sandwich is killing me."

"And now it's killing me! Roll down your fucking window, you disgusting Slavic bastard!"

Before he does, Putin slams Vassy in the upper arm, and then aims his hero out the window like it's a laser pointer, "Our Professor!"

Squinting as he scans the streets, Vassy takes a second to locate their target as he rubs the pain from his arm, "Where? Holy shit! Did they already settle their score with the poor bastard?"

Vassy's quick appraisal of Professor Dunlop's business dealings is based on Dunlop's strained stride, which is hampered by a severe limp, making his pace appear frantic. Sadly, for Dunlop, the only thing that has kicked his ass so far, has been his poor planning. Since abandoning his ride, Dunlop has exasperated the left leg injury he suffered when pushing his ride to the pump, by maintaining a brutal pace to the port. His dated and dilapidated dress attire makes him appear destitute and somewhat demented. Furthering his disheveled appearance, sweat stains pooling from his crotch look more like poor bladder control, than a poor choice in wardrobe. The only body part that looks to be more uncomfortable than his damaged leg is his head, which swivels, scans, and shakes whenever one of his hands finishes wiping a clump of sweat-soaked hair from his face.

"Don't know if it's a settled score or a birth defect, but it hurts to watch," Putin remarks with genuine concern.

"Did you see him get out of his car?" Vassy asks as he scans the humid horizon.

"No car. He limped here," Putin confirms.

"Come on. From where?" Vassy questions.

Smiling as he continues to monitor the Professor's pained progress, "You can't see that far, because you're probably older than the artifact he's smuggling."

Rolling his eyes, Vassy quips, "I can see where this is going."

Putin drops his half-eaten hero and grabs the radio, "I'll call it in. HQ will—"

Vassy's hand wraps around Putin's, with a speed and strength that betray his fat, feminine physique. "No—wait."

Searching Vassy's starving stare with skepticism, Putin asks why.

A small smirk curls Vassy's pouty Puerto Rican lips, "Trust an old timer on this one… It's about to get a whole lot more interesting."

# Chapter 4
# A Name by No Other

Your name is actually three names: your given name, aka, your first name, your middle name, and of course, your surname, aka, your last name. In many cases, all three names have significant meaning and in others, they're somewhat meaningless. You were named Jonathan, in honor of your Uncle Johnny, while your middle name is Phoenix, because your father said that when you were born, he rose from a drug-induced death spiral and became a new man, stopping the booze for an entire week.

Nicknames, on the other hand, are a little different... Though they can carry some historical significance, or character trait, they're more often than not an affectionate way to shorten your given name. Robert becomes Robbie. Maybe a baby brother couldn't pronounce Nancy, and said Nannew instead. To this day everyone in the family calls Nancy, Nannew, and reminisces around the holidays about how cute Nancy's baby brother, now the size of a refrigerator, was for not having age-appropriate linguistic skills.

A stage name is an attractive sounding name that has more to do with one's desired professional persona, than their actual personality. Rich Evans, transforms into Richard Events. If his film career goes into the crapper, which most likely will be the case, he may do drugs and porn, and subsequently change his screen name to Dick Evenings.

An aviator's call sign is a nickname that's a healthy mix of Hollywood showmanship and brotherly love—an attempt to add some levity to the serious business of strapping fuel and explosives onto your person, and flying twice the speed of sound into death's embrace. Given to the pilot by a commanding officer, or a fellow rocket jockey, the name should embrace the pilot's most endearing characteristics, or reference something the pilot has done of noteworthiness. Overly macho, or mockingly feminine, call signs trump all prior names given an individual, for it's the first name the individual has actually earned.

If you decide flying isn't your thing, and instead of banking high-speed rolls, you'd rather bank rolls of cash, you may choose to be a mobster. In that case, instead of a call sign, you'll one day earn a made name. A made name veers off course from all other names an individual may be known as, for one simple reason: the person who gives it to you may not even know you. Maybe they've never even seen you. They certainly don't have to like you, especially if it's a holier than thou reporter at some liberal rag, wanting to make a name for himself, more so than you.

Regardless of whether it's a reporter, cop, victim, competing crime Family, or the head of your Family, the name is always for a reason, some more apparent than others. Do you kill a certain way? Do you dress a certain way? A cross between a stage name, a nickname, and the name your great-grandfather was given at Ellis Island based on his craft, a mobster's made name can be equal parts respect and ridicule. In the end, just like a team's record, you deserve your name, whether you like it or not. Whether a name is a good fit is irrelevant. What matters most is that your name carries respect when said, and that you're prepared to do the heavy lifting to carry it forward.

The name Tommy Two Touch was both earned and respected. No one mocked Tommy. No one… Not anyone in the competing Families, not anyone in the police department, and certainly no one in his own Family. Tommy got the name for one simple reason: if he needed to touch you a second time, it was usually going to be the last time you were touched by anyone. More legend than reality, Tommy would make it a point to punish in public to keep up with perceptions. Tommy was naturally a people person, but knew fear and intimidation were tools of the trade, and a job could only be as good as the tools used. Therefore, Tommy mastered his craft while maintaining a tidy toolbox.

When Tommy was twenty-two years old, he was already overseeing the muscle side of the management team that ran cigarettes from Columbia, South Carolina to Hackensack, New Jersey. Interstate trafficking anything that fell under the ATF, was both profitable and combustible—as in, the entire operation could blow up in your face at any moment, for any reason. Managing a ten-rig trucking and fulfillment business would have been stressful enough had it been legitimate. Add jail or death to a missed shipment and an employee severance package could include a severed head. Needless to say, issues went sideways in a hurry. If one of the rigs got pulled over, the chase vehicle had only moments before the reporting officer made the final call to the precinct, thus the powers that be had to decide whether to treat the officer like a lamb, or a pig.

Should a driver decide he was going to retire off a "lost" shipment, one had to make sure he was found along with the loot and made an example of before the entire fleet drove into the Bermuda Triangle of trucking, aka Jersey City. The reoccurring inter-office snafu wasn't an easy fix, for drivers weren't lone wolves like most of the employees or shop keeps who were controlled by the Mafia. Drivers fell under an organized Mafia that dwarfed the families they worked with. The Teamsters were a union of super bad-ass mother fuckers, comprised of ex-bikers, ex-cons and falsely documented workers, who collectively answered to no one, but their union representative. They were the blood of the U.S. Interstate arteries; therefore, if you wanted a transfusion, you'd better have a doctor's note. Just as sick and vacation days were accrued and used unconventionally, employee morale and motivation were handled differently than they would be in a Fortune Five Hundred company. For all intents and purposes, Tommy was a Mafia HR department, handling employee issues, whether they had an issue, or they were the issue.

The complaint department was also a one-man show, run by Tommy's boss, Manny Vaciano, aka Manny Hands. Manny was given the nickname 'Manny Hands', simply for the fact that he continually had his hands in many different things at once. A great delegator, Manny excelled in project management before the title was even coined by big business. Manny wasn't as fortunate as he was hardworking, for he'd found himself on the wrong side of a drive-by shooting in 2001, and had been unceremoniously re-nicknamed 'Manny Holes' by the crime Family who'd gunned him down. That assassination kick-started a three-year turf war that resulted in the consolidation of the lower Bronx garbage routes, which, in turn, compelled the very grateful, Godfather of the Catanzano crime Family to bestow upon Manny, at his funeral, his last of many nicknames, 'Manny Routes.'

In one such scenario, Manny had informed Tommy that the truck driver who went off the radar three days earlier had been spotted at the local strip club, The Felt Pelt. The Felt Pelt was a retro dive where over-the-hill strippers and aging hookers could work for peanuts, without concerning themselves with physical conditioning. Management didn't shy away from their dried-up talent pool, but rather embraced the lack of talent and proper hygiene, deciding on the name, The Felt Pelt, to promote the fact that the women never shaved their privates.

Years later, the club was remodeled and renamed The Boxed Lunch to appeal to the growing business lunch crowd that was popping up near the new football stadium. The impromptu renovation was oddly enough indirectly funded by a Saudi Prince who had come to the establishment by chance on his way to Atlantic City. He happened to have two obscure fetishes that crossed streams at The Felt Pelt: pubic hair and mature women. Finding himself on his knees, trembling at the front door, pitching a tent, the Prince offered to pay every woman working ten thousand dollars to shave their beavers, in addition to compensating the owner of the club a million for his troubles. Rumor has it, he took the hair back to his country and had an afghan rug woven from it, where it adorns the floor of his personal ten-man submarine, The Muff Diver. What isn't rumor is what the owner did with the Prince's money. The next day he fired every old hag he had, and spent half the money remodeling the place, transforming it from a dive to a destination. As the last nail of the remodel was hammered, so was the last nail in his coffin, for he'd spent the other half of his million on blow, which lead to a fatal heart attack on the eve of the grand opening. The owner's untimely death was responsible for the joint's current nickname, The Box, which was actually short for the full nickname, The Pine Box.

Tommy had arrived at The Felt Pelt just as Jerry Timmons was leaving with a fellow driver. Both men were clearly inebriated, obviously oblivious to Tommy's existence. Tommy, of course, was straight as an arrow, and saw them as soon as they stepped foot outside of the club, even though he was in the process of stepping out of his own car at the time. It didn't take him long to scan the lot and see their rig parked off to the side, hidden in the shadows. Tommy strode briskly between the cars, intending to cut them off right before they entered their rig, consciously keeping his stride short, which slowed his pace just enough as to not garner their attention.

By the time Tommy intercepted them at the front of the rig, Jerry had already taken his dick halfway out of his pants and was pissing in a lazy zigzag pattern as he smoked a butt he'd kept clipped to his ear throughout most of the evening's festivities. His over-the-road teammate, aka his co-driver and partner in crime, Joe DeSimone, apparently had forgotten to take his dick out and was currently pissing in his pants as he complained of his wife's cooking as part of an incoherent babbling bitch session. Joe was a lazy, good for nothing, piece of crap. Making four times the money than a legitimate driver, Joe blew his wad and dick five nights a week in holes littered along Interstate 95, only to come home and slap his wife while screaming in a tirade to his two toddlers that no one understood his pain. Tommy would have wanted to knock Joe out if they had simply bumped into each other as complete strangers on line at a coffee shop. The fact that Tommy knew his history and his poorly planned future, made this the easiest employee intervention of his career.

Literally bumping into Tommy in front of the rig, Joe stumbled back a couple of feet, slowly reacting to an obstacle that he hadn't predicted being there. Tommy took advantage of his momentary lack of focus and struck him with a vicious right windmill that was only made possible by Tommy's insanely thickly muscled and properly positioned lower body. Crumbling to the ground unconscious, Joe fell awkwardly, collapsing like a high-rise building in a controlled demolition. Whereas the hundreds of tons of free falling steel and concrete would be too much weight for the lower floors to hold, Joe's three hundred plus pounds of roadside beers and burgers were too much for his unconditioned, atrophied trucker legs to withstand, causing one side to buckle backwards, resulting in the lower-left leg bone snapping from its connection at the knee. The snap of the bone, the thud of the body on the ground, and the rip in the jeans, through which the bone now protruded, told Tommy all he needed to know—Joe was no longer a threat.

Jerry Timmons was about as ready for a fight with Tommy that night, as he was for a stripper to offer him a free night of lap dances. He staggered back at the sight of his buddy, and made a series of uncoordinated gestures as he couldn't figure out whether he should turn and run, or put his pecker away and zip up his pants before he swung for the fences. The result was similar to a receiver, who, for the life of him, couldn't figure out whether to catch the ball first, or turn and run with the ball he hadn't caught yet—a fumble. As Jerry fumbled with his penis and positioning, he began to fall backwards over his half-raised jeans, resulting in Tommy being touched in a fight for the first time in two years. Adding insult to injury, it wasn't Jerry's last-ditch left, or an accidental karate kick from a flailing leg that struck Tommy, but rather a stream of urine that flew upwards as Jerry fell backwards. The arc of acid laid a machine gun'esk trail of reddish-hued urine drops on Tommy's white suit that ran from his crotch to his chin, with the last drop shooting up Tommy's left nostril. The urine was hot, wet, and smelled of cabbage and bad beer. Tommy, who had stopped drinking five years earlier upon the birth of his first son, Timothy Frances, immediately halted his advancement to assess the total damage.

Shocked and enraged, Tommy attempted in vain to gain control, via a calm and controlled breath he'd begun practicing since his first bout with asthma at the age of eight. This time, much to the dismay of Tommy and, in turn, Jerry, taking a deep inhale through his nose had the complete opposite effect he'd intended. Whether you're throwing deep down field, or snorting air up your nose, a long, powerful, committed delivery allows zero room to stop your action mid-motion, thus Tommy was subjected to the sensation of the pee drop entering his nasal passage as it cooled, only to warm again as it was exposed to his body's inner temperature.

A thousand snapshots of Jerry's disgusting lifestyle flashed before Tommy in rapid succession, from an undisciplined diet, to unprotected sex with crack whores with AIDS. To Tommy, the drop was literally poison incarnate, a violation and staining of his body, mind, and soul. Whatever effect the drop had on Tommy's inner being, the outward effects were instant and horrifying, making one think he had inhaled a deadly cocktail of testosterone, acid, and bad Chinese food, for Tommy transformed into a mobster version of the Incredible Hulk before Jerry's bleary eyes.

No longer caring for the condition of his brilliant white suit and pearl white Italian leather loafers, Tommy leapt onto Jerry like a rabid baboon, slamming a knee into each of Jerry's kidneys. What remained of the urine within Jerry's dick, subsequently shot up like a geyser, directly up Tommy's crotch and back, enraging Tommy even further.

The first punch that hit Jerry was so powerful that it not only broke his nose and left cheekbone, but the subsequent impact of his head bouncing off the hard-packed dirt was enough to fracture the back of his skull as well. By the fifth punch, Jerry was a vegetable. By the tenth punch, Jerry was dead. Though Tommy didn't know he'd killed Jerry at the time, he knew something had been altered significantly within Jerry, once there was no more bone left in his skull to resist his fists.

Tommy quickly looked up to see if there were witnesses, and to his surprise there were two truckers no more than fifteen feet away, frozen in the shadows. Tommy needed to assess the situation rapidly. Looking to Jerry, he knew Jerry was either dead or at best, in need of serious medical care quickly. He halfway turned to his original hit, but heard the distinct moans of a drunk waking in writhing pain, and knew he'd most likely bleed out due to the bone's break and the booze-thinned blood if the wound wasn't cauterized sooner than later.

Tommy jumped off of Jerry and bounded a good three feet towards the men, while simultaneously pulling his .45 Magnum, nicknamed Redwood, after the custom-made redwood handle Manny Routes had commissioned for him after a very successful business transaction.

The men froze in fear, with hands raised in front of their faces as if Tommy was pointing a flashlight at them instead of a gun.

"Move and die! That simple, Gentlemen," Tommy stammered out of breath.

Tommy knew he had only seconds before more truckers poured out of the club, or a State Trooper pulled up. He had to dispose of all four of these guys and the truck before anything was missed.

"Empty your pockets!" Tommy demanded.

The two men were slow to respond, but after Tommy closed the distance and waved his gun close enough to the taller man's face that he could feel the cool breeze of the barrel, both men began to frantically empty their possessions. Once Tommy saw what he wanted to see, which was their cellphones and ID's, he ordered them to step back. Once again, they were slow to respond, but it wasn't out of a lack of respect, but lack of composure, and Tommy was seasoned enough to know the difference.

Tommy directed them rather patiently on how many steps they needed to take, and once he was satisfied, he gracefully gathered the pertinent items – two cellphones and two ID's, purposely leaving the loose money and other belongings on the ground. Tommy walked backwards to his two hits and rummaged through their personal effects, finding both their phones and ID's.

"Come here," Tommy demanded.

The two men slowly walked to him.

"Closer," Tommy instructed.

The two men walked to within two feet of Tommy, before Tommy raised his gun in their direction and switched his aim from one face to the other several times.

"Now, you're going to put these two deadbeats in the back of the cab."

"How?" Asked the short, chubby trucker with a mangy beard.

"First you're gonna pick them up one at a time, together. Then I'm gonna open the door and you're gonna lift them in nice and gently and lay them on their beds." Pointing with his gun to the 1997 plain white, International double cab they stood in front of, "The cab is a double sleeper isn't it?"

Both men nodded.

"OK then. They need assistance and rest, so you're helping me help them. You ready to be good Samaritans, or are you going to try to be heroes?"

Both men looked lost.

Tommy overly exhaled and fluttered his eyes to show annoyance for their ignorance, "A good Samaritan would help me, while a hero would cry for help. See the difference?"

Both men looked at Tommy with wide eyes and then to each other for an answer. Their lack of comprehension and composure was just as unsettling as understandable, so Tommy tried one more time, before he shot twice and did all the heavy lifting himself.

"You gonna try, or ya gonna cry? 'Cause I'll tell ya right now, nobody likes a cry baby." Tommy finished the sentence with cocking his gun and pointing it at the taller of the two men.

Both men answered with a jerky unsure shoulder shrug and nod, which was good enough for Tommy.

Tommy used his gun as his director's wand, pointing to his new partners in crime as he gave them orders, "You, grab him by the shoulders, you by the legs. Chop, chop."

The men went about their grisly task with only a quick delay at Jerry's body to take a breath and assess the technical aspect of lifting the dead weight. As the men moved the bodies, Tommy had regained his full composure, and was no longer reacting out of instinct alone, but was also applying his years of street knowledge and counterintelligence to his exit strategy. He removed the truck's CB and scanned for any other devices that would allow someone to communicate with the outside world, specifically law enforcement, while driving the truck unsupervised.

While the men loaded the second body, Tommy perused through their personal effects and found what he was looking for, a picture. A picture-perfect family that one of these guys cared deeply for. So deeply that he made the conscious decision to live and work inside a 6' x 6' box on wheels, for eleven months of the year, with another smelly, hairy, sweaty bald bastard, to make sure they had all they would ever need.

As the men lowered themselves from the truck, Tommy made sure to compliment the one driver on his family, "Wow, what a beautiful family. I bet you can't wait to see them again."

The taller driver's eyes widened as he stumbled forward with animal rage and fear, but stopped himself dead in his tracks as Tommy raised his gun to his face. Tommy made sure to assuage his fears, with the game plan. "You help me, help others, and I'll help you get home to your beautiful family, a happy and healthy daddy. Capiche?"

The tall driver nodded slowly, as he tried to make sense of Tommy's elongated innuendo. Tommy decided to emotionally connect with his hostages, making himself seem somewhat human. "I also have three kids, with my little one being born just two months ago, so I know how important family is to a dad, and how important a dad is to his family."

The driver gave a slight jerk of his head and momentarily closed his eyes, possibly trying to hold back a whimper.

"You're gonna drive the truck and follow me. You understand?"

"Yes."

"Good. You." Tommy pointed at the shorter man with his gun. "You're gonna drive my car. Capiche?"

"Yes," the shorter man with the mangy beard responded softly.

"Good. Let's roll."

As the men began to walk to their driving positions, Tommy made sure to set the tone and record, "Remember Gentlemen, I already gave these guys a chance, just like I'm giving you.

They blew that chance, and now it's yours. Don't blow your chance."

The drivers who had already begun to walk to their respective vehicles had their backs to Tommy, and Tommy took advantage of their compromised positions, reaching out and anchoring his massive meat hooks on both men's shoulders, stopping them dead in their tracks. "Before you drive, a tip to stay alive. The first time I touch you, it's a warning, the second time, isn't."

The drivers did not turn their heads to Tommy, nor even bob them in acknowledgment of the warning. And it was only after Tommy broke contact that the men even began to breathe, let alone move. As the men walked to their driving positions like the robots that would one day replace them, Tommy made a short, coded call to alert the other party to their impromptu rendezvous.

The drive was almost as short as the call, ending abruptly a couple of exits down the Turnpike, in the worst area of Jersey City. The byproduct of big ideas and premature political promises, was a stretch of rundown industrial buildings located underneath a tall stone bridge that spanned marshland and wasteland alike. As they approached a dilapidated, trash-lined fence, surrounding a nondescript, abandoned warehouse, a well-dressed man appeared from thin air and opened the gate, which moved more smoothly along its tracks than one would expect. The car and truck drove through the yard at a pace that suggested Tommy knew where they were going and knew nothing would impede their progress along the way. As they arrived at the run-down shell of a building, the large rollup door rapidly retracted, exposing a pitch-black interior.

The car pulled in fast, stopping as hard as it had accelerated, resulting in squeaking tires that sent echoes throughout the empty facility. The repetitious chirp alerted their unseen host of their arrival like an expensive doorbell. The truck followed suit, and once both vehicles were inside, the door closed faster than it had opened.

Once inside with nothing more than the headlights on, Tommy tapped his horn four times. On the fourth tap all the lights in the warehouse went on simultaneously. Huge halogen lights made the night, day. The truckers and Tommy had to take more than a moment to adjust to the new view. The warehouse was pristine inside. A freshly mopped, newly set slab of concrete led to walls that were bare except for the reinforcements and thick soundproofing material that made the place more fortress than lean-to. There wasn't even shelving, or stacked boxes to make one think it was used for anything other than this one moment. Adding anxiety to the intrigue that the truckers were surely experiencing, were the blacked-out windows located at the top of the walls. To the outside world, this warehouse hadn't been occupied in years and no one was about to check on its availability.

Two men approached the vehicles from each side, totaling four. As Tommy began to exit the car, he motioned to the driver to do the same. Once Tommy and the driver were clearly out and about, the tall truck driver with the cute kids joined them without Tommy's direction. Scanning their potential executioners like birds pecking bread crumbs in a park full of kids, the drivers huddled close to Tommy with their backs to each other.

"Strip and ship fellas," Tommy said in a softer tone than expected. The walls were high, metal, and empty, and thus despite the cheap, foam soundproofing, his voice reverberated throughout the facility.

None of the workers gave the truckers a second look, and began taking the two victims out of the cab without further ado.

"This one's dripping!" A loud voice from within the cab exclaimed.

Tommy looked to one of only two doors in the place, "Hey, cement stains! Time's ticking! Chop, chop!"

The door swung open and three additional men emerged. The one in front was decked out in a stylish silver silk suit, similar to Tommy's, while the two men behind him wore what appeared to be workout outfits underneath translucent, plastic body shells, with plastic booties covering their sneakers. Each plastic clad worker pushed a dolly carrying a large, black, metal drum. As the well-heeled man approached, a large stack of money could be seen clenched in his left hand, while his right gripped a light gray canvas tarp.

As the men approached, Tommy motioned with his chin for his guys to move away from the truck with him, clearing the way for the new three.

Upon arrival, the man in the suit tossed the still folded tarp to the ground and walked to Tommy. As he went to hug Tommy, one of the two plastic men picked up the tarp and began to unfold it next to the driver's side door.

"Save the salutations until I change," Tommy said to Manny as he pointed to his piss-stained suit.

"What a shit show," Manny said as he assessed the situation and Tommy's suit.

"Whatever happened to professionalism?" Tommy asked no one.

"Lucky for you, laundry arrived earlier today," Manny said to Tommy.

"I got church today," Tommy said absently.

"There's a nice light blue suit there. You treat yourself well, my friend," Manny said with outward affection.

Tommy smiled softly and Manny turned to address the new guests. "You two know why these guys are at the end of the road?"

Neither man spoke and only broke eye contact with Manny to look to Tommy for their answer.

Tommy took their silence as a respectful acquiesce and decided to throw them a bone, "Because Gentlemen, they were trusted and then broke that trust. They were treated very well, and in turn, treated those that treated them well, terribly. Now what's befallen them is terrible. Capiche?"

Both men nodded vigorously to acknowledge their comprehension and acceptance of their fate.

"I'm sure Tommy's told you how we work around here. We reward hard work and loyalty, while punishing lazy, greedy traitors."

Both men nodded again, but it was when the father of the cute kids witnessed the two lifeless former employees being unceremoniously transported into their final rest stop that he had an epiphany, solidifying Tommy's nickname and countless tall tales that would soon follow, "You'll never have to touch me twice Tommy, I swear on my family. Never again Tommy. One touch is all I need. God's witness." At this point all the men were out of the vehicle and heard the prophetic promise.

Manny nodded in approval and handed Tommy the wad, which was actually two wads. Looking to the two new truckers, Manny forewarned, "Tommy Two Touch is a great boss to have. You're rather lucky to have stumbled upon such a golden opportunity. You'll both retire early, with your children's colleges, along with your family's house, paid for in full by this very man." Putting a warm hand on Tommy's shoulder, "That said, the job's for life and you'll decide in the end how long that life's for. Capiche?"

Both men blinked heavy, weary lids, then said yes. Tommy turned to the two new employees and handed them the wads. "Pleasure doing business with you gentlemen, and I look forward to working with you in the near future."

As both men took the money, Tommy asked them, "What do you do when someone hands you five thousand dollars?"

"Thank you," both men said softly and sincerely.

"Actually, it's a trick question. Rhetorical if you will. You see, if someone hands you five thousand dollars, you've already done something." Giving a quick grin, "But you're welcome, nonetheless."

Tommy then reached out to put a reassuring hand on each man's shoulder, to warmly welcome them to the Family, only to have both men cringe and step back slightly, as if Tommy was about to touch them with a taser gun. "Fellas? Don't be so uptight. You're family now. I don't hurt family... Unless I got to."

Both men eased up somewhat, acknowledging Tommy's good nature with tired, fragile grins, which were the windows to their souls. Tommy's empathetic eye bore deep into the shattered windows, viewing the carnage of their random voyage. Holding his thought, as he held their gaze, Tommy knew the faster they got on the same page, the faster they could turn it, "Remember, if I gotta really reach out and touch you, you'll know why, and instead of handing you a wad a' cash, I'll hand you a shovel and make you dig your own grave. Capiche?"

"Yes Tommy," both men uttered.

"Good," Tommy said approvingly. Turning to Manny Routes, "What's say I buy you a cappuccino and cannoli at De Lillo's?"

"Tommy, I love you, but it's 4:30 in the morning. They don't open 'til seven on Sundays."

"I'm not sure when they flip the sign in the window, but they start baking at five, and they open when I get there," Tommy said matter of factly.

# Chapter 5

# Partners in Crime

The worst part of the Bronx is worse than one can imagine, and Tommy was currently deep in thought, imagining worst-case scenarios. This was going from a shit show, to a shit storm, and when things went from bad to worse, Tommy needed to know his out. And in order to figure out his out, he needed to understand what he was in—in trouble was the easy answer, but what went wrong and why needed further evaluation… Why he'd agreed to pick up The Razor in the first place was something that had his instincts questioning his sanity. Duty, that's why. The duty that a Family's faith and the absolute trust in a brotherhood bestows upon you. Even when those same obligations mean doing right by your own, means you'll be doing something that doesn't seem quite right. Right now he needed to trust that his bosses wanted him to pick up The Razor and take him to a job, rather than what his gut was telling him, which was that he was delivering the job to The Razor.

The streets near the old docks were dirty and dilapidated. In worse condition than the aging infrastructure from yesteryear, were the homeless vagrants that littered the alleys and abandoned buildings, who lived in constant fear. To the languishing lives that were worth less to society than the trash they used for shelter and sustenance, acts of atrocity were merely tools of the trade to a group of humans isolated from humanity. Less than thirty minutes from the center of the world was Hell on Earth, and Tommy was about to meet The Devil himself.

+ + +

As Tommy's loaded and pristine 2013 Cadillac DTS with a flawlessly waxed, tri-coat, sky blue aftermarket paint job and handcrafted java leather interior, flown directly from the craftsman himself in Grosseto, Italy, slows to a crawl in front of the old meatpacking plant, where The Razor received his guests, a thought flashes like a switchblade in an alley altercation. The Razor loved to live among the walking dead, because it not only made his job easier, but frightfully fulfilling. By living inside a nightmare, he could live a lie and con his conscience into believing that all life wasn't worth living, thus easily ending it.

Thinking of the children you're currently chopping up, giggling in their backyard, as their mom, whom you just tore the flesh from, bakes a cherry pie in the same kitchen you're currently using as a processing plant, would drive even the insane to madness. No... Rather, think of a junkyard full of people who would prefer death, rather than another day of dying. In that world, The Razor's world, he was God, not the Devil. In Tommy's world, that made him even more dangerous...

The plant hadn't packed a piece of pork in fifty years, but Tommy knew The Razor processed meat there on a regular basis. Not the Kosher kind, mind you, the human kind. It was rumored that The Razor took his most prized catches here to work them over, before he chopped them up. During the weekly card game, a Wise Guy by the name of Bobby Bombay, once told a harrowing tale of accidentally surprising The Razor at the plant, only to find him boiling a huge stew in one of the massive old cauldrons left over from the packing plant's heydays. He swore he saw a finger rise to the top and that he only noticed it, because it had a gaudy, gold engagement ring on it. When he asked The Razor what he was doing, The Razor told him, God's work; even going as far as comparing himself to Robin Hood, but with a gruesome innuendo. "Whereas Robin Hood stole from the rich to feed the poor, I simply feed the rich to the poor."

Bobby Bombay, whose last name was actually Devine, was given Bombay as his nickname due to the bizarre side effect that quinine in tonic water had on his penis. At an important family wedding while Bobby was in his twenties, the connection was made that drinking gin and tonics resulted in a massive boner, and some levity was desperately needed to excuse his social faux pas on the dance floor, involving the bride and her mother.

The night of the wedding, as with the night at the card game where he told the tale, Bobby drank himself into oblivion. This time though, instead of nursing a hangover for a week, he offed himself a week later with a shotgun at his hunting cabin in Downsville, NY. Everyone knew the shotgun was too long for Bobby to suck and blow simultaneously, so when the head of the Family said cowards kill themselves, everyone knew the hit was sanctioned and forgot his name and all his silly stories.

Now parked out front of the plant, Tommy surveys the scene, turning his head slower than he wants, using the mirrors more than the windows. The windows are bulletproof, of course. The extreme cost of the windows had turned into a far less frivolous purchase over the years than the hand-sanded teak wood inlays, that the former owner had commissioned from an artisan having trouble making his interest payments. *No one pays off what they owe*, he thought. *How in the world can you plan for the future, if you're always paying off the past?*

Tommy lived in the world of all cash. His cars and house were paid in full, as were his kids' college tuitions, even though the oldest was too young to understand what attending college would mean to both himself and Tommy. In addition, Tommy's family was guaranteed a comfortable life, based solely on his legitimate businesses and real estate holdings that spanned two coin-operated laundromats, a bowling alley, a deli, and three gas stations, as well as a five-story, medium income apartment building, all located within walking distance to his beautifully manicured, Greek revival home, which abutted the nicest section of Pelham Park.

Death didn't frighten Tommy, but that didn't stop him from taking plenty of precautions to cheat it. His favorite ride, a triple gray CTS-V, had a couple of aftermarket extras, over and above the bullet proof windows and level-three stage ballistic armor plating that were standard fare for someone of his station. The most outrageous of which was a system that rapidly deployed razor sharp stakes from the seat cushions, with a push, or pull of a foot lever located next to the hood release. If he pulled the lever with his foot, the back seats would be activated, jettisoning stakes from both the seat bottom and back. If he pushed the lever, the front would be activated, exploding the headrest, with the majority of the blast directed towards the windshield. The maker of the self-defense system was adamant that the driver understand there would be some collateral damage with the headrest detonation, but that installing a spike system was not an option, due to the space already required to house the mechanical innards of a heated and cooled, 20-way adjustable seat.

He was told by the installer that if he needed to do both, he should pull first, for it may be difficult to pull on the lever once it was fully depressed. Tommy thought it was better to pull first as well, but for tactical reasons. His thinking, if the guy in the front was just killed, and Tommy was temporarily incapacitated due to his proximity of the blast radius, it would give the guy in the back more than enough time to off Tommy, considering his gun was most likely trained on Tommy since entering the vehicle. Furthermore, the guy riding shotgun would be performing his part, acting nonchalantly for their fellow motorist and law enforcement, while giving Tommy driving directions, or more likely than not, a sermon on why Tommy was in his current predicament. Regardless of what he was saying or doing, he wouldn't be focused on what was going on in the backseat, thus affording Tommy the element of surprise.

Who he killed, in what order, never materialized, and Tommy never even tested the system since its installation, due to its onetime use and extremely expensive replacement, similar in scope to an entire system of airbags being deployed. The system's exotic, deadly nature, coupled with its lack of a proper testing and track record, made Tommy uncomfortable transporting his family in the car on Sundays to church. To assuage his fears, Tommy purchased the Cadillac DTS, which had been upgraded to level-two ballistics by its former owner, who ironically, was shot and killed in the car while parked with the windows down during the hottest day of the summer. Tommy had mused on several occasions that the poor soul should have invested in a stage two air-conditioning unit as well.

Unfortunately for Tommy, though he purchased the DTS with the ballistics upgrade already installed and subsequently commissioned the car with the creature comforts of a luxury liner, he hadn't thrown down any coin on a self-defense system, such as the one in his CTS-V.

Angry with himself for not making the obvious car swap on his way to Killville, he awaits The Razor, agitated, brushing his sole against the lever that isn't there. He knows he's close, for he can feel his angry eyes, over the dozen sets that were currently starving on the street less than a stone's throw away. Tommy scans his side-view mirrors and sees nothing new, but knows The Razor has somehow positioned himself within striking distance, for the homeless near his car have stopped moving. Frozen with fear, they stare to where they know eye contact won't be established with the predator they pray to.

Tommy takes a long deep breath before peering into his rearview mirror to see who he is. *Time to shine* he reassures himself, as his tired, dry throat collapses momentarily under a mountain of neck muscle. A hard gulp, made possible by a flexing Adam's apple, supplies enough saliva for Tommy to smirk at the sucker sitting behind the steering wheel. Motion from the passenger side mirror draws his attention, where a standing stone-still Razor meets his gaze with contempt. *How did he get all the way to the rear passenger side door undetected? I'm either off my game, or he was hiding in the sewer drain. Thank God I locked the doors when I got off the exit.* A curt nod from Tommy acknowledges The Razor. Unlocking the doors is all the welcome he'll get. The Razor struts forward, a cat on a fence, opening the door and entering with an effortless elegance Tommy assumed would be mutually exclusive of a 6'6" skeletal frame.

Fixing his jacket, The Razor is all business, "You're late."

"Official business with the Boss runs la—"

The Razor cuts him off faster than his last victim's head, "The Boss called me thirty minutes ago and said you were en route."

"I had to make a stop," Tommy elucidates.

"Where?"

Looking out the window Tommy looks for a ruse, "Your wife's. Close the door."

Closing the door, The Razor looks in the newly positioned rearview mirror, "I killed my wife on our wedding night."

"Cold feet?" Tommy remarks.

"We're late. Drive."

Tommy gets tense from the tart reply, "Relax Pal, we'll get there when we ge—"

"Shut up," The Razor chastens.

Tommy hadn't let anyone but Ellie speak to him like that since Father Joseph caught him smoking on school grounds in middle school. "Shut up? Are you fucking nuts talking to me like that?"

The Razor isn't fazed by Tommy's outburst, "I'm nuts alright. And if you don't shut up and drive, I'll cut yours off and feed them to my friends."

Shaking his head in utter amazement, "What's with the nuts and this Family?"

Smirking, as he scans the entrance to an alley forty feet from the front of their bumper, "I'm not your family."

Puffing his chest out further than his chin, Tommy displays defiance, "You don't scare me with your dark talk."

"Yes I do. I'm a scary person, Tommy. Because, not only am I nuts, I'm evil. And to make matters worse, I truly want to kill you."

"Feeling's mutual," Tommy retorts.

Taking a moment to process Tommy's admission, The Razor's rebuttal is meant to rile, "Yes, but no."

On cue, Tommy seethes, "Come again, Crazy?"

Amused, The Razor muses, "You want to kill me, but for a different reason..."

"You're an asshole?"

Smiling despite himself, The Razor articulates, "Your desire is based on survival. Quite natural actually... Your primordial fear is a manifestation of your desire to protect yourself and those you love. Nothing to be ashamed of, but certainly not worthy of boasting."

Tommy purses his lips, "And why do you want to kill me? 'Cause I was late?"

"I want to kill you for the pleasure. I want you to feel pain and misery, fear and loss. I want you to cry, while you die."

The Razor is outwardly enjoying fracturing Tommy's façade and Tommy is painfully aware of it and resents it. "In the end, if I kill you, you're dead too. Same results... Big deal."

The Razor locks his all-knowing eyes on to Tommy's, "You've never killed someone before, have you?"

Though The Razor's eyes were colder than a witch's tit, they ignite Tommy, "I'm a made guy, Pal—and your superior, may I remind you. I've done what needs doing. Trust me, I've been around the block."

Sneering at Tommy, The Razor's retort spews sarcasm and spittle. "You've been around the water cooler with the other liabilities, exchanging fairy tales of bravado."

Rolling his eyes, Tommy's tense tone betrays his cavalier critique, "I get it. You're the natural born killer of the Family. The black sheep in a wolf's den. No need to get nasty. We're all professionals."

"I'm nasty, Tommy. That's my profession."

"Right, right. You're the ultimate badass. The Boss loves you. Thinks you're gonna make everything just right tonight."

"It warms my heart to know the Boss has such confidence in my abilities," The Razor unempathetically utters as he scans their rear once again via the passenger side mirror.

Tommy decides his noncommittal comment was an opening to opine, "Personally, I think you're more bark than bite, and your drama isn't needed for this situation."

But Tommy goes too far, and knows before it finishes flying free of his mouth barrel that the shot off The Razor's bow was more brazen than brilliant. The Razor's pupils refocus on an ongoing internal dialogue, and he's more than just a little combative, "Situation... situation is it? That's what you believe this is?"

Stammering, Tommy knows he'd sounded silly, "It's not that big a deal. The Boss has lost more money at the track in one afternoon. We'll get most of it back anyways. Besides, I'm gathering you'll make a fucking mess of the poor guy and all will be impressed when your handiwork is on the morning news."

Folding his hands in his lap, The Razor poses a question that Tommy hadn't asked himself, "What if he's talked to someone already?"

"So?" is all Tommy can utter.

"So?" The Razor rebukes, somewhat taken aback. "So, you messed up Tommy. You compromised the Family. Word on the street is we got played by some washed-up nobody. Families will be curious as to what's happening inside the ranks that allowed this to take place. The Family is now vulnerable from all sides. Our resolve will be tested, and it won't be pretty."

Wrenching his sweaty hands tightly together, Tommy doesn't know whether to pray with his hands, or start punching himself in the head, "I fucked up. I got it! What now? You gonna kill me too?"

"Not yet…" The Razor answers academically.

With baited breath, Tommy asks, "When?"

Shrugging, The Razor seems to genuinely contemplate the cutoff date, "Not sure."

With the realization that he was a legitimate hit, Tommy's vision blurs slightly, as the blood that was trapped within his clenched heart, under unfathomable pressure, bursts from the seams, filling his head, until his eardrums pop. Waiting for the tide of blood to subside, Tommy clears his throat in hopes of pushing down the remaining pool of pain, before addressing the five-hundred-pound gorilla in the car, "The Boss told you to whack me?"

As if Tommy had asked him whether he wanted extra cheese on his slice, The Razor deadpans a 'no'.

Like a desert flower forming from the first spring sprinkle, Tommy's soul instantaneously rejuvenates, coalescing colorful commentary. "Thought so! I'm a Made Guy, you psycho fuck! You kill me without consent, and the entire Family will come after you! No stone unturned, Pal!"

"I have no family, Tommy. Unlike you…"

"You threatening my family you cocksucker?!?!?! That's the second fucking time you brought up my family. You mention them a third time and I'll spray your fucking brains against that window!"

Displaying his irritation openly, The Razor decides to lecture instead of listen, "When the Boss is sick and tired of someone's incompetence, or he just wants to cull the herd, he sends me."

"Regardless of who orders it, I've got people I'm tight with within the Family. They'd respect Ellie's wishes, but they'd take vengeance on you in a heartbeat. You'd spend the rest of your short-ass life, looking over your shoulder! I can promise you that."

Sincerely smiling, The Razor sets Tommy straight, "No one will really look for me after I kill you. You know that, don't you? They'll say they are while at the bar as they toast your life, but only in hushed tones, after making sure all ears are pointed elsewhere. No one will really want to find me. I'm the story that the old man is always trying to bury. I'm the necessary evil that keeps him up many nights, but yet, helps him sleep through others. He's tied to me more than you will ever know."

Sneering as if he's smelling The Razor's rotted soul, Tommy gives him a once over as he levels, "You skeeve me out."

Once again, The Razor doesn't bite, but rather gives Tommy something to chew on, "It's your natural instincts kicking in, Tommy. Your subconscious knows I want to do you harm, and it's trying to protect you, but you're too stupid to listen to it. It's telling you to run. Take your wife and children and flee the Bronx."

Clenching his fists, Tommy's neck veins look like exposed roots on a Japanese maple, "Fuck you! You want to kill me, go ahead! Let's do this, Razor! Right fucking now! Take your best shot. I'll rip your fucking head off your shoulders!"

Tommy's sorrowful attempt at an impenetrable wall of wails is nothing more than a thin veneer over fear to The Razor, "You're petrified of me."

Tommy doesn't know whether to cackle in his face, or to spit in it, "Please!"

"Your heightened fear, heartbeat, sweat, are tangible treats to my senses. If it helps you to concentrate on driving, you've been granted a short stay of execution."

Once again taken aback by The Razor's cavalier comments on his life expectancy, Tommy is forced to ask the obvious, "And why should I trust you?"

Now it's The Razor's turn to act astonished at the other's ignorance, "I don't have a driver's license. I need you to drive me to and from the meeting."

"So, you'll kill me, my family, and a man you've never met before, without a moment's hesitation, but you won't risk breaking the rules of the road?"

"Precisely."

Shaking his head slightly, Tommy tries to process the nonsensical statement with the same difficulty as he'd experienced when his oldest son had said that one day he'd be an LA Dodger fan, "You're even more fucked up than I thought."

Once again rolling with the punches, with a guy who's got no plans to pull one, The Razor keeps an emotional detachment that would make a kindergarten teacher envious. "I'm good at killing, which you'll fully appreciate sooner than later. Driving? Not so much… Plus, I've been caught driving with a suspended license twice, while I've never been caught killing someone."

"So, you kill—" Tommy pauses while he processes the gravity of what The Razor openly admitted to, "Because you're good at it?"

"Abraham Lincoln once said, 'Whatever you are, be a good one.'"

Caught off guard by The Razor's reference, Tommy quickly reengages with cynicism, "You're a big fan of Abraham Lincoln, are ya?"

"I'm a big fan of anyone who considers a million dead, a means to an end."

As if he were speaking to the dive's designated drunk, Tommy orates the obvious, "He saved the country."

The Razor clarifies his beliefs even though he knows full well Tommy wouldn't understand him, let along believe him, "He delivered a pipe dream by actualizing it at all costs, which places him in rarified air, especially since it was on a global stage that eventually affected every person on the planet."

Pursing his lips, Tommy raises an exaggerated eyebrow, "And the connection betweens the two of you is?"

The Razor smiles broadly, betraying his current mood, "I'm not making any parallels between us… Just a fan, that's all."

Scanning The Razor from head to toe, Tommy rests his eyes on The Razor's lap, where a large black top hat rests, "Is that why you wear all black and that stupid hat?"

Looking down at the hat fondly, The Razor taps it gingerly, "Actually, yes."

Tommy pulls his eyes from the hat to scan the street, "You don't think that makes you stand out?"

Brushing the brim with the back of his thumbs, The Razor whispers, "It does indeed..."

Directing his glare back to The Razor, "Wouldn't it behoove you to be a little inconspicuous while walking around a crowded market, looking to kill someone holding a giant gold artifact?"

Purposely avoiding eye contact, The Razor remains focused on the hat's elaborate stitching, "You know the Boss sent me here, because he wants the world to know who, what, when, where, and why."

Tommy's glare transforms into a scowl, "And of course, tomorrow's news will fill the airwaves with how."

A knowing smile widens on The Razor, as he assesses the outcome of his next admission, "My passion for my craft will ooze through the screen, Tommy. Granted, most will be disgusted, but in the end, it will resonate with enough…"

Now literally sick to his stomach, Tommy does a double take of The Razor before asking, "Resonate? You mean to inspire others to kill?"

The Razor looks up from his hat and out the front glass. His stare is distant and strangely serene, as if he were fondly recalling a childhood crush, "Not to kill, but rather inspire others to do great things, or at least do things with greatness."

"Inspiration, passion, dedication to one's craft... You're a real beacon of light for today's youth in an otherwise bleak socio-economic picture," Tommy states with heavy sarcasm.

Smiling absently at the prophetic picture Tommy has accidentally painted, The Razor closes his eyes, noticeably relaxing his posture, as he inhales deeply, seeming to bask in the warm glow of imaginary sunlight, "The doom of a nation can be averted only by a storm of flowing passion, but only those who are passionate themselves can arouse passion in others..."

"More Lincoln?" Tommy asks annoyed.

"Hitler," The Razor responds as he opens his eyes wide. Dusting the cobwebs of a dream, The Razor looks ahead, focusing on a point somewhere beyond the event horizon. Squinting as if the object of his affection has become obscured by the bright light of the beyond, The Razor becomes terse in his talk, "We're late. Drive."

Tommy shakes his head, drops the car in drive, and locks his lead leg.

## Chapter 6
## Risky Rendezvous

By the time Professor Dunlop arrives at the market, he's physically and mentally exhausted. Just being on his feet is a testament to his newfound tenacity, and Dunlop makes sure to take a measurement of his manhood, finding himself rather smitten with his metamorphosis. As he takes stock, he finds solace in knowing that the old Dunlop, even a twenty something year-old version, in top physical conditioning, couldn't have covered the distance in the time he'd just accomplished it, let alone done it with the jarring injuries he'd sustained prior and during the epic marathon. Since starting the harrowing trek across the Bronx, he'd received more bruises, honks, and curses from his fellow Bronxites than in the prior ten years combined.

In addition to pulling up with a lame leg from pushing his car into the gas station, Dunlop had been clipped by a taxi and decimated by a full-frontal collision with a food delivery man on a bicycle along the way. Running full tilt into the rusted red Schwinn at top speed had resulted in Dunlop flipping over the handlebars end over end, landing several feet away, mildly concussed. Though his forehead looked as if he'd taped a shitake mushroom to it, it was his right shoulder that had taken the brunt of the impact, resulting in a massive contusion that now limited the arm's range of motion.

To add insult to injury, upon getting to his feet, Dunlop was immediately body-slammed by a good Samaritan, who assumed Dunlop had stolen something from someone and believed it to be his civic duty to detain Dunlop until the proper authorities were notified. After several minutes of the older, heavier man sitting atop Dunlop's back, awaiting police assistance, Dunlop persuaded the vigilante and bicyclist that he was just an idiot. Before freeing him from his body shackle, the good Samaritan, along with the bicyclist and an old Asian lady who'd been standing on the corner hocking individually wrapped roses in clear plastic cones out of an old mop bucket, teamed up to deliver a come to Jesus dress-down, which included everything from advice on being a better person, to getting his hair cut short enough as not to obstruct his view. When Dunlop was finally able to stand on wobbly legs, he noticed much to his dismay that he'd not only torn his suit pants at the knees, but had torn the flesh from both palms.

Now staring at open, bloody palms in the middle of the loading lot, Dunlop is transfixed by not only how far he's come, but how far he's fallen. His two open and empty hands remind him that he'd left his briefcase at the curb where he needed to recover from the taxi hit and run. Disheveled and destitute, sweating profusely through his cheap, worn and torn gray suit, his hair a mess, the bloodied and bruised Dunlop looks to have just survived a plane crash in the jungle. Looking up to the loading docks, he sets his shoulders, breathes deeply, then exhales slowly as he straightens his jacket. Before hobbling to his rendezvous point, he makes sure, out of habit, to button the jacket's top button.

His limp is so pronounced, it borders on the theatrical. Severely paranoid of both being caught and being late, Dunlop continually looks over his shoulder as he pushes a painful pace. Intense pain and physical exhaustion make his erratic, uncoordinated, jerky movements along the loading dock resemble that of a pirate captain with a wooden peg for a leg, pacing the aft deck, as her Majesty's Royal Navy gains ground.

Completely out of his element and mind, Dunlop unwittingly bumps into several dock workers and stationary crates as he stammers forward, desperately trying to locate his rendezvous point.

Finally, finding the Italian flag protruding from an old wine barrel, ten paces past the last of the nineteen heavily-trafficked bay doors that comprise the main loading center for the 1.7 million square-foot Hunts Point Market, Dunlop finds himself bordering on hysterical. Though still in one piece, he's broken, and not knowing who his contact is, or why he's not currently there, are just as mentally and emotionally taxing, as the trek to get there had been physically.

Was he too late? Did his contact get cold feet? Was the whole operation a lie, and he'd just pissed away his last chance at breaking even? Worse even, what if it was legit, and his contact had just been killed, or cuffed by the cops while waiting for him. Was he next? He couldn't imagine how bad his mug-shot would look if it was taken now. Would he allow himself to be taken? If he'd paid his whole life policy's premium, instead of letting it lapse like his car insurance, he'd at least be worth more dead than alive and could hang his hat on going out with a bang… At least he wouldn't have to face the music, or worse, his kids.

As thoughts race through Dunlop's mind, even faster than Dunlop had raced across the Bronx, a dock worker thumps into him, knocking him almost over the barrel he was using as kickstand. Forty-something, heavy set, South American, and donning a blood-stained smock over work jeans and a tattered T-shirt, the man who almost finished Dunlop continues on his way towards the corner of the main warehouse, as if their contact was casual.

To Dunlop, his actions were outrageous, "Fucking Christ!"

The man stops several feet away to inspect an eighteen-wheeler's trailer, checking a box on a clipboard after each approving nod. Turning in the general direction of Dunlop, the man says in a thick Argentinean accent, "Follow me. You're late."

*Our jostle wasn't an accident!* "Where?" Dunlop questions.

"Move now. You're drawing attention," the man hisses as he continues his quick pace along the platform. Somewhere between his early forties and late sixties, Edgar is a hardened, first generation Argentinean, commercial butcher, who's received more knife wounds over the years, than the cows he'd cleavered.

As Dunlop begins to follow Edgar, the excruciating pain overcomes his ability to keep up and shut up, "Slow the fuck down please!"

Edgar keeps walking at his usual all-business pace, scanning the area for prying eyes.

"What's the rush?! It's an antique, for fuck's sake. Fish go bad, not antiques!" Dunlop whines.

Dunlop's inability to follow basic business protocol peeves Edgar, but he refuses to lessen his powerful, short stride, "The antique might not have a shelf life, but this deal does."

Literally on his last leg, Dunlop has no choice, but to openly plea his case, "Please! For the love of God, I can hardly walk!"

Edgar comes to an abrupt halt, tilts his head back, and exhales a long, frustrated breath, while forcing his large oven mitts to his kidneys, as if the posture would force the last of the air from his body. Forcing Dunlop to hold his breath, while he holds his pose, Edgar finally pivots with the melodramatic motion of a movie star, and is dumbfounded by Dunlop's catastrophic condition. "My God! What happened?"

Flabbergasted, Dunlop screams a whisper, "I told you I can't walk!"

Looking in every direction he can without moving his head, Edgar is still in a state of shock that Dunlop is walking, let alone talking, "Why didn't you mention this on the phone?"

"It happened on the way here," Dunlop exhales.

"You were attacked? Why didn't you call?" Edgar implores.

"I wasn't attacked. Sort of…" Dunlop says as he rubs the temples of his head with closed eyes.

Still scanning Dunlop in utter amazement, "What then? Car accident… Shit! You file a police report?"

Voicing his displeasure at the new line of questioning that clearly cannot correct the calamity of the circumstances, "No! We're good. OK?"

Edgar doesn't continue his line of questioning, but levels him a skeptical stare.

Dunlop tries to assuage his fears with some much-needed levity, "The only report I'm filing is the one with the Better Business Bureau on the store that sold me these shoes, okay?"

Edgar, who is still sketching visuals for the storyboard that explains Dunlop's disheveled state, is caught off guard by his declaration, "Pardon?"

Pointing to the ground, "It's my shoes… They're not made for walking…"

Edgar is at his wit's end with Dunlop, "Are you fucking with me, Mister?"

"No."

Edgar puts a frank-sized finger to his graying stubble, "Who buys shoes not made for walking?"

Shaking his head, Dunlop is outwardly irritated by the indignation of yet another dress down, this time from someone who's never even dressed up, "They're dress shoes."

"So?"

"So, they're made to look good, not feel good," Dunlop quips.

Unaware of Dunlop's disingenuous dissertation, "Don't they make shoes for both?"

Edgar's honest inquiry destroys Dunlop's deceitful dialogue, "None that I can afford…"

"Why did you want to look good for our meeting?" Edgar pries, somewhat mystified.

Beside himself, Dunlop can't help but be sarcastic, "I wanted to make a good impression? Who the fuck knows?"

Edgar, clearly not satisfied with the Q and A, decides it's go time, by motioning Dunlop to follow with a toss of his chin in the direction they need to head. Momentarily overjoyed by Edgar's new, slower pace, Dunlop is dropped back to Earth on his ass, by Edgar's assessment of his situation, "Your cover is already blown. You're being watched as we speak."

Flustered by the revelation, Dunlop is quick to dismiss, "Impossible!"

Edgar doesn't turn, so Dunlop can only imagine the smug smirk Edgar's fat face flaunts as he philosophizes, "Impossible? You're picking up an ancient artifact at a wholesale market in tap shoes."

"Who followed me?" Dunlop demands.

"I'm not sure who followed you here, but there are two undercover cops staked out front since lunch," Edgar states.

"They could be here for any number of reasons," Dunlop argues. "Isn't this the smuggling port for the Northeast?" he adds rhetorically.

As Edgar peers around a corner upon entering the warehouse, he quickly looks back over his shoulder at the door from where they'd just come inside, and mutters under his breath, "And the gateway to the West for all things nefarious."

"I'll keep that in mind after I cash out," Dunlop deadpans.

A slight of build, twenty-something, Central American man jogs up to Edgar, and whispers some Spanish slang in his ear. Edgar, whispers back and then slaps the man on the shoulder, "Vámoose!" Turning to Dunlop, Edgar's face flashes from white to red, then white again, before going back to its native color.

Dunlop can't read his expression, but knows the story's genre isn't comedy. "What?" Dunlop asks expectantly.

"I hope your transaction is C.O.D., because two guys showed up right behind you and they're apparently from another Family."

"Another Family?" Dunlop inquires.

Shaking his head in utter amazement at Dunlop's ignorance of the severity of the situation, Edgar cannot help but sneer as he speaks, "There are two families that run this market, and it's understood that no one else shows up unannounced."

"Maybe they're here for the fresh produce?" Dunlop clumsily concludes.

Edgar begins to move again down the box-lined hallway, this time the pace is somewhere between the first time and the last time, "These guys are looking for something, but it ain't produce."

"What did they look like?" Dunlop asks.

"The driver was a short stocky guy, with blond hair thicker than his arms. He's muscle, no doubt. The other... My eye said he looked like he just stepped out of a horror flick. Tall, thin, white skin, straight long black hair, black suit and a fucking top hat?" As Edgar walks, he looks up and off to the distance as if the last detail makes its mark on a memory.

Blowing hard enough to flap his lips, Dunlop admits, "I think I know the driver."

"Who is he?"

"Tommy."

"Tommy got a last name?" Edgar annoyedly asks.

"Calls himself Tommy Two Touch?"

"Tommy Two Touch? Are you fucking kidding me? Oh my..." Edgar's voice picks up speed along with his pace.

Dunlop begins to strain to keep up, but is more concerned about what Tommy will do to his leg, than what the walk will, "You know him?"

"He works for Catanzano."

Dunlop knows the name well, "Catanzano financed the deal."

Edgar stops in his tracks, spinning to Dunlop, "You brought a Catanzano transaction to this port? You fucking insane?"

"What's the big deal? Business is business, right?"

Edgar, shaking his head in disgust turns once more and begins to walk, as he scans the rafters, "This port was won with blood! This port is heavily guarded. This port might as well be filled to the fucking brim with TNT and you've just arrived with a lit match."

"I'm sure things aren't that bad," Dunlop says with little fanfare, as he peers over Edgar's shoulder.

Edgar slows considerably as he approaches a corner, where crates block the view from afar, "You have no idea what you've done, nor what you're in store for?"

"In store?"

Edgar turns to Dunlop before moving ahead, "You're a dead man walking."

"What did I do?" Dunlop whines.

Edgar shrugs his shoulders as he tucks something under his shirt, "No idea. But if Catanzano is willing to risk an all-out gang war, he's already on the war path..." Edgar stops dead in his tracks, "Dear God!"

"What?" Dunlop screams as he walks into Edgar's back, crumpling like a Ming vase slamming on cement from the penthouse patio.

"The guy with the top hat…" Edgar trails off as his eyes go wild.

"You know him?" Dunlop anxiously inquires.

"Yeah… that's got to be The Razor," Edgar sadly states.

Noticing Edgar's angst, Dunlop asks a rhetorical question he'd prefer not answered, "That's bad I take it?"

Looking off in the distance and then turning to Dunlop, "It won't end well if they get you."

Seeing the severity in Edgar's stare, Dunlop loses his cool, "I don't get it! I promised to get his money back as soon as I sold it! I told him he could bank on this one! Bank!"

Breathing heavily through his nose, Edgar reflects on what would happen next, "He's settling all accounts now."

"I have kids—a wife for crying out loud!" Dunlop declares.

"Now'd be a good time to call them," Edgar offers.

Absently brushing his empty pockets, Dunlop mutters softly, "My phone's dead…"

As Edgar resumes his endgame, Dunlop follows suit, but with an energy level lower than his cellphone's, and a heart aching worse than his leg. Wishing he was still back at the gas station with his crappy car and phone, he starts suffocating under the weight of his actions, and it's a strain to just stand. "Wait…"

Edgar stops, but doesn't turn. Raising his head back, he closes his eyes, as he gentle drops his hands into his smock's deep pockets. Stretching his Adam's apple, he braces for Dunlop's bitching.

"Wait! Please!"

Edgar doesn't turn, but doesn't move. Both men remain stationary like the crates surrounding them, awaiting their fates and final destinations. Finally, Edgar's left arm mechanically raises from his side, leveling straight from the shoulder. He points into the dark distance he fears to peer into.

"What? Out with it. I've got no time for games!" Dunlop protests as he begins to trip towards his tormented guide.

Edgar remains nothing more than a signpost until Dunlop literally grabs his arm demanding answers. "What are you pointing at?"

"The crate in the corner," Edgar absently answers.

"It came in that?" Dunlop questions cautiously.

"What is it really?" Edgar enquires, as he musters the inner strength needed to rotate his head towards the crate.

"You don't want to know," Dunlop abhors.

"It's cursed, isn't it?" Edgar asks.

Sighing heavily, Dunlop confirms Edgar's worst fears, "Yes..."

Edgar spits to the ground and steps back, still looking to the crate, "The rats don't even go near it. Not even the fucking flies... Every time I walk by it, I get goosebumps and my heart aches." Fixing his stare on Dunlop, who's fixated on the crate, Edgar execrates, "It's evil."

Not looking to argue the obvious, Dunlop decides it's time to move, "I better get it and bail."

"Where to?" Edgar asks.

Dunlop runs his hand through his hair in hopes to jump start his memory, "There's a park around here. It's old. Near the water. I'm to make the transaction there. Do you know where... Pelham Park is?

Edgar glances back to the crate and exhales through sucked cheeks and circled lips, "It's a walk. I'm not sure in your condition you can make it. How big is the object? The crate's large."

Visualizing what's inside the crate other than the scepter, Dunlop appears even more confused than scared. "It's not big... It's just a knife..."

"Just a knife?"

"Sort of... It's a scepter. A symbolic weapon of sorts."

Still keeping his eyes pinned to the crate as if it could leap in the air at any moment and rip his throat out like a savage animal, Edgar doesn't appear too taken with the extended explanation, "Over there... There's a crowbar in the corner. Take whatever it is and go down that hallway. Third door on the right will lead you to a back-alley. From there, take care."

"Thank you," Dunlop utters with great sincerity.

Still eyeing the prize, Edgar is resolute and resigned to the ramifications of both his and Dunlop's actions, "Don't thank me; leave. I'll do what I can for you, not because I like you, but because any blood shed here will start a three Family gang war."

"If this object falls in the wrong hands, a much bigger war will start," Dunlop declares.

"How do you know the hands you're delivering it into are the right ones?" Edgar questions.

Shaking his head slightly with his eyes closed more from fatigue than fright, "I don't..."

## Chapter 7

## From Bad to Evil

Though the savory symphony of pungent cheeses, sweet peppers, and spiced meats produced prodigious pools of saliva in Putin's mouth while he waited on line at Mario's, and the sensory explosion induced while he mangia-ed it down later in the car were nothing less than a porno for his palate, the subsequent smell of the fire's smoke that now lingered, mingled like a recluse with the car's preexisting nauseating odors of farts, cheap cologne, cigars and B.O., making the stale air stymieing. Arguing useless points on topics you didn't have a horse running in, with a person you didn't respect, was painful at best. Arguing with said person, while his breath held repulsive notes of wet onions and soured mayonnaise, made one wish the conversation were over a phone, not an arm rest.

"Don't think for a minute birds love!" Vassy shouts as he squeezes a wad of his shirt over his heart.

Not perturbed by Vassy's rage, Putin speaks quite eloquently for someone talking out of his asshole. "Not only birds, but all reptilians."

Looking to the smoke-stained felt roof of their broken down undercover cop car, Vassy is flabbergasted, "I thought you were retarded when I first met you, but I clearly overestimated you."

Stuffing the last of his sandwich in cheeks so packed, he resembles a puffer fish defending itself, Putin sucks each fingertip of his right hand like a baby sucking its pacifier, before he garbles a retort with a mouth full of food, "Whatever makes you feel better about eating them."

Turning from the ceiling to the idiot, Vassy is now just as confused as annoyed, "Who the fuck eats reptiles?"

Believing his useless information is actually fascinating factoids, Putin pushes the point, "Ever have frog's legs?"

"Frog legs? Who the fuck would eat that shit?"

Seemingly shocked by Vassy's dismissal of a delectable delight, Putin opines, "Aren't you from a rainforest?"

"You have got to be shitting me…" Vassy utters, astonished.

Fluttering his eyes closed, Putin's patience finally falters, "Don't give me the insensitive bit, you little—"

Raising his hand to Putin's mayo and mustard-lined lips, Vassy is finally able to convey why he's been stunned to silence, and it's surprisingly not by Putin's stupidity. As he murmurs the words, "You have any idea who that is?" he leans forward and points with his other hand until the tip of his left pointer finger touches the windshield, creating a sweat-soaked circle.

"Getting out of the car?"

"Yes!" Vassy exclaims.

"Which one?"

"The passenger. The passenger!"

Scratching his head, Putin draws a blank, "No, but get a load of the hat."

"That's The Razor! The fucking Razor!"

Rather than satisfying the itch with the scratch, Putin momentarily moves the memory further back in his forehead, "Pardon?"

Looking to Putin, Vassy squints, as if the sun, not rage is blinding him, "The Razor? Jimmy "The Straight Razor" Schiavetta? You're a fucking detective in the Bronx, working homicide, and you don't know the craziest killer to ever walk the streets?"

"The hitman?"

As if Putin had answered the last question right on Family Feud to win their family a vacation to Puerto Rico, Vassy explodes, "Yes, the hitman! The genuine fucking article in the living flesh. Or maybe not… How the fuck can white people, be so fucking white and still be alive?"

Putin rolls his eyes, "And I'm racially insensitive."

"Shut the fuck up! We got to strategize." Frantically scanning the car, Vassy locates his cellphone resting on his seat between his crotch and checks it quickly before tossing it into the cubby hole under the ashtray in disgust. Peering out the rearview and side mirrors, Vassy seems to sense something building only seconds away from transpiring, "Now!"

Taken off guard, Putin tries to defuse the Dominican, "Chill, hombre…"

"Don't 'hombre' me. Seriously, never."

"I called you my friend."

"I hate when white people try to talk ethnic. It's insulting."

"Sorry muchacho."

"This changes everything. We've got to move, and move fast."

"What does it change?" Putin inquires with genuine interest.

"For starters, the life expectancy of our Professor."

"Why?" Putin prods.

"Why? You really live in fantasia. That's Jimmy "The Straight Razor" Schiavetta—okay? And Catanzano keeps that freak behind glass, and only breaks him out when the shit hits the fan."

"Why did the shit hit the fan?"

"Why did the chicken cross the road? Who the fuck knows! What I know is The Don only uses The Razor when he's either settling a score or sending a message, or both."

"He's a bad ass, huh? What'd he do again?"

"What'd he do? What's he not done? He's a sicko. A bona fide psychopath."

"And you're sure he's not here for intimidation? Maybe The Don wants to send a message to the other Families?"

Mystified by the meathead he must address as partner, Vassy squints in apparent pain, "Like what?"

"Like, don't do business with guys that are shoving their dicks in my ass…for starters," Putin orates.

With his last thread of patience fraying, Vassy bloviates, "You don't get it, do you? The Razor has one message, and one message only. You fucked up big time, and now your time is up."

Somewhat skeptical, Putin probes, "Then why isn't he running the show? It's no secret Catanzano could use some added muscle, especially on Arthur Ave."

"Most of The Don's Wise Guys, including his lieutenants, are petrified of The Razor."

"Are his killings that effective?" Putin questions.

Somewhat more in control of his disdain for his partner's ignorance, Vassy decides to enlighten him, instead of berate him. "Effective? Bro. He not only kills the victim, but the family as well. And brutal slayings to boot—fucking brutal."

Deflating in to his seat as he stares straight at The Razor, Putin burbles, "Sounds crazy…"

Seeing that reality is finally sinking in, Vassy dials the volume down another notch, but keeps the rhetoric levels at ridiculous, "Quintessential crazy Papi. As in, Jack the Ripper crazy, i.e. he uses melee weapons exclusively."

"Melee?" Putin inquires.

Shaking his head at yet more inexcusable ignorance, Vassy states what should be the obvious to a detective in the Bronx, "Knives, shivs, razors, swords."

"Swords?" Putin repeats in disbelief.

"Fucking swords," Vassy confirms.

"Morbid…" Putin mutters.

Exhaling allows Vassy to pull his gaze away from The Razor, and set it on his partner, hoping the severity of his stare will sink in, "I've seen him do a Zorro in one Wise Guy's pregnant wife. His kill-style even has a nickname in homicide."

Grossed out, Putin's attention has officially joined the stakeout, "Come on!"

Seeing the floor is now his, Vassy holds a second for the drama to build, "When a kill matches his… they call it a Pot-sticker."

Putin grabs the holy shit handle above the door and cringes before he notices his reaction. "Why isn't he in jail? I mean, he's killed so many times he's got his own call sign?" Forcing himself back into his seat and his hand to the arm rest below the window, Putin continues with a contrived condescending quip to portray a calmness he cannot hope to achieve, "Sounds like legend and lore. Does he ride a dragon when he's not carpooling with a goon?"

Vassy knows his audience is hanging on his every word, regardless of the posturing, "All gore, no lore. Hundred percent evil."

"Fuck me…" Putin whispers as he sinks into his seat despite himself.

Seeing his words had literally settled in, Vassy wants to see if Putin is on board, "So you get what's next?"

"What?" Putin responds, perplexed.

"What do you mean, what?" Vassy snaps.

"I mean what, what!" Putin counters.

"I'm going to take care of business. That's what's what!" Vassy voices. "You got a piece?" He adds with a voice reserved for a library.

"Pardon? Piece of what?" Putin asks.

Put-off by Putin's posturing, Vassy fires sarcasm, "A piece of shit! Don't get cute! You got?"

Putin may not be the brightest bulb in the chandelier, but the lights are on and someone's home, "In the trunk, passenger side, up, back, and taped behind the speaker."

With Putin on board, or at a minimum, not looking to jump ship anytime soon, Vassy regains his composure, "Good. Now how do we set this up?"

Putin might not be looking to walk the plank, but he wants to make sure the captain knows he can swim if needed, "Whoa compadre... I'm not killing anyone. I got a good thing going."

"You? You're staying here and eating your sandwich. I'm taking this cocksucker out solo," Vassy states.

"Hey, we're cops. Remember? We don't get involved in this shit. Think for a sec."

"I'm thinking crystal clear," Vassy declares through clenched teeth.

"Maybe you think so, but cops don't kill without cause," Putin protests.

Looking at Putin with utter contempt, Vassy contends, "Cause? You need cause?"

Stuttering, Putin looks to calm the rhetoric and his own nerves, "Some... Some more than your opinion of his mental makeup. For if that's a death sentence, you better buy more bullets Pal, because we've got a long night ahead of us."

Unmoved by Putin's diatribe, Vassy lays it out, "How about this. Once this little bust of ours is made public, we'll be the ones responsible for putting the kibosh on Mr. Crazy's kill, and he comes looking for us."

"You think he'll come for us?" Putin whimpers.

"I'd be shocked if he didn't. And remember, he doesn't just kill you, he kills your family first."

As Putin slumps back into his worn-out, no-frills, cruiser car seat, like someone gazing into a moonless night, he's brought back to his front yard, where he was lucky enough to be groped in the wee hours of the morning, by possibly the prettiest lady in all the Bronx. Adding an MVP trophy to the Super Bowl victory, was that the lady happened to be his pregnant wife, who in her third trimester, could leap like a lioness off the front steps and catch him in three strides, before he escaped in his squad car. Making sure he had a snack and his workout bag, she was every guy's dream girl, a pin-up poster body, housing a heart the size of the Jersey shore and a brain sharper than a razor... The Razor he laments.

Suddenly, a vision of The Razor walking up to his front door and methodically knocking until his wife answers it, paralyzes him. He snaps to from his disturbing daydream before seeing whether she lets him in. He'd seen enough, which meant even though he didn't agree with his partner on why, where, and when things should be done, he knew now that things needed doing. And like his amazing partner in life always preached when she bid him farewell before a new shift, "Do the things that need doing." Finishing the statement with a long and powerful kiss that at the end, she'd somehow symbolically sucked out of his mouth all the anxiety, anger, and apprehension he was experiencing. His wife wouldn't want him to kill The Razor per se, but she'd be more than happy to exchange The Razor's life for her children's absolute safety. In the end, that was the selling point. Need, not want. Sure, he wanted things, but those things would come in time. He needed to know his family was safe. "You think killing him is the best course of action? What about the Catanzano Family coming after us and killing us just the same?"

"First off, no one's gonna kill us like The Razor. Shoot me ten times, before you stick me in the belly with a shiv. And no one else in the Family would dare cross the line of offing our families."

"All actions have a counter," Putin remarks.

"All upside my friend. With The Razor gone, the Catanzanos will breathe a collective sigh of relief."

Caught off guard by the new revelation, Putin sees a glimmer of hope, "Wait! They'll be okay with this? Taking out their hammer?"

"The Don might be upset at first, 'cause The Razor's his blow, but his Underbosses will let him know he's better off," Vassy denounced.

"An Underboss happy with the loss of the ultimate weapon?" Putin inquired.

"They'll be more than happy with his death, for he's a wildcard, and doesn't answer to anyone within the Family, including The Don, to be frank. No one in the Family trusts him: The Don less than any of them," Vassy lays out emphatically.

Blowing softly out of puckered lips, Putin attempts to comprehend the Catanzano's conundrum, "Sounds like a powerful addiction The Don's got. Afraid to turn your back on the only thing that's got it."

"The other crime Families are absolutely petrified of him, and what's more? His death would be a boon for law enforcement," Vassy adds with enthusiasm.

Resting a thoughtful hand to a brick chin in contemplation, Putin tries to reason insanity, "So the law wants us to snuff a citizen without even so much as a trial?"

Sensing Putin is shitting the bed, Vassy pontificates, "Do you have any idea how many guys on the force have information one way, or another on something, but have The Razor's fury in the back of their heads as their reasoning for not breathing a word?"

"Wow. You've really have thought this out," Putin harps.

"Joke all you want, but this would be the best thing for your career, since you accidently saved that boy from drowning."

Putin remembers the day like it happened yesterday, and is convinced he'll never forget a frame—a moment that saved both the boy's life and his career. Putin was going nowhere fast, and the girl he loved since training wheels, was hightailing it out of town.

Disenfranchised, he'd been playing hooky from work, jogging along the beautiful beach of Pelham Park, debating his future and mustering enough meaning in it to warrant sticking it out in a career that failed to fulfill, when a motion in his peripheral vision slowed his stride. The splashing among the thick, green, bay grass that had caught his attention turned out to be another lovesick lad playing hooky, and not an egret fishing for frogs.

The short of it was, the kid was a punk, and a dumb, lazy one at that. He was also high as a kite and had booze on the breath to boot. Putin knew he'd been drinking, because he had to perform mouth to mouth in order to save his life. And though Putin may have been slow to seize some opportunities, he was always fast on his feet when it came to capitalizing on commotion.

When things got crazy, Putin got cool. It was his trademark since the first window broke due to an errant swing in stickball. Thus, before the paramedics showed, he decided to assess the ass he'd just saved. The boy's clothes said money and the bottle of **Ladyburn Legacy** single malt, said the money was old. Which is why Putin chose to interrogate the boy before the first flatfoot arrived, and in doing so discovered that not only were his parents rich, but politically powerful.

Giving the boy advice on what to say to whom, Putin took the ambulance ride to the hospital, even meeting the parents in the waiting room before they spoke to the reporting officer. Reporting the naked truth to them, he decided on a revised one for his Sergeant and the local media. The story of a young, athletic officer patrolling the seashore and subsequently saving the life of a curious kid, looking for samples for his high school science experiment, saved the father's political career and pole-vaulted Putin's. Overnight Putin became a celebrity, which was something special before the advent of the Internet. Armed with political clout and a career offering endless possibilities, Putin was invited to every social occasion imaginable that the Bronx had to offer. Of course, he needed a trophy-wife hanging from his arm to properly enjoy the moment, and being that he was already in love with one, next steps happened swiftly.

Smiling fondly at a game well-played, Putin is more than happy to hear Vassy out, "How so?"

"You'd be promoted, made, and knighted with one pull of the trigger. You'd be fucking untouchable by dawn."

Weighing the pros and cons that came along with being a professional con, Putin had a knack for seeing the light, even in the darkest hour, "A win-win…"

Nodding with a smile, Vassy is emphatic, "Every Family from the Bronx to Philly would be indebted to us, as well as every major police organization that couldn't solve a case, 'cause someone held back info."

Snapping out of his daydream, Putin patronizes his partner, "You're doing this for notoriety?"

Hurt by the innuendo, Vassy refuses to vacillate, "I'm doing what needs doing! It's a thankless job, Putin, so you need to seize your raisin-in-the-sun moments when they present themselves."

Set on his decision well before Vassy finishes his closing argument, Putin is already focused on the bigger picture, which is why he had leap-frogged his petty partner long ago, "If that's the case, why don't we concentrate on the loot?"

Arching an eyebrow of approval, "Now you're thinking like a Special Prosecutor."

Relaxing like he'd sunk into a recliner, Putin smiles at the windshield as if he's watching the Yankees celebrate another pennant, "Special Prosecutor Putin… I like the ring to that."

# Chapter 8

# Dunlop's Debut

The crate is harder to pry open than a nun's legs at Easter Mass, but Dunlop finally separates the lid with his soul's last sip of strength. As the last rusted, bent nail snaps to attention, the lid flies back, thumping dust into the air as it skids to a stop a couple of feet from the base. As the dust settles, Dunlop finds himself grabbing itchy nostrils, as he musters the internal fortitude needed to peer into the abyss. The box pulsates a putrid power, but Dunlop finds himself basking in the grimy glow. He doesn't know if what's in the crate has his head pounding, or what's left in his heart… A humming noise, similar to a broken florescent lightbulb ballast, increases in both octave and cadence. Dunlop knows the noise isn't natural and that it's emanating from the crate and not the ceiling.

Firmly planting both palms on the crate's rim, Dunlop's grip grows with intensity until the back of his knuckles turn white. Holding onto the box with outstretched arms, not sure if he'll jump in or push off, he lowers his head for a final thought. Without knowing if the water is ice cold or boiling hot, he takes the Nestea Plunge, pulling his head over the edge, as he forces his tightly clamped eyelids open. Lying cattycorner in the 5' x 5' crate is a long, black and gold shaft, adorned with enormous emeralds the size of deep sea oysters. Roughly cut, their designs look chaotic, but their arrangement on the shaft and head are not entirely random. The head of the stick has a circle of gems wrapped around it. The amount of light the semi-sphere collects, even within a deep-walled crate, which is hidden in a windowless back room is not only astonishing, but very well could be physics defying!

Dunlop lunges for the booty, but quickly retracts his hands, as if he senses the scepter's hidden boobytrap. Contemplating his next course of action, he surmises that whatever boobytraps were set to guard the treasure had been sprung long ago by the tomb-raider who stole it. Satisfied with his initial safety concerns, he's still having a tough time of convincing himself that the coast is clear. *You'll be fine. Stop being such a massive pussy for once in your Goddamn fucking life! Just grab and go! Don't over think this, just do this!*

When Dunlop's internal clock counts to three, he forces his hands down into the crate. The five-foot drop to the bottom causes him to leave his feet and contort his body over the edge. Upon grasping the rod, Dunlop finds himself teetering on the top of the crate. Taking a moment to compose himself, he acquaints himself with his newly-prized possession. It's not heavy, but seems to be firmly planted on the crate's base—by what he doesn't know, for he cannot see any cable system tethering it. Conventional wisdom would suggest something would have been used to keep the extremely old and most likely fragile artifact in place, so that it wouldn't be damaged during the long journey. But yet, there didn't seem to be anything holding or protecting it… Astonished, Dunlop forgets his fears for the moment, and yanks the long pole up, but instead of following him out of the crate, it's Dunlop who comes crashing down inside of it.

Slamming into the same shoulder that had been decimated earlier in the day by a collision with a bicycle, the pain is almost too much to bear. Fighting desperately to stave off his body's internal defense system, which currently wants him to pass out, tears run down his cheeks as his bottom lip trembles. On the verge of an all-out toddler tantrum from the pure frustration of the day and his current circumstances, Dunlop finds his face pressed against the cool, hard handle. Having no choice but to readjust himself within the crate, Dunlop decides to take the jolt of pain he knows will come with applying the additional weight on his shoulder, in order to right himself. Caught between a rock and hard place, Dunlop mans up and makes the move, wincing as he flips over.

Once over, Dunlop finds himself straddling the scepter. His fear and fatigue are inexplicitly replaced by anger and oddly, exhilaration. *You're mine! Stop fucking with me and do as you're told!* Dunlop grabs the scepter, and lifts it up. Momentarily stunned by the ease at which he has lifted the object that mere moments ago defied physics, Dunlop accidentally bangs his balls with the scepter as he rises from his knees. As he erects himself, he brings the scepter forward, holding it straight up. It's ice cold. He can feel the heat dissipating from his hands, and instinctively knows that the heat will be used to create an ambient temperature for himself and the scepter. Neat…

Short on time, Dunlop knows he cannot study the artifact in the crate, but gives it a first blush anyway. Taking note of the massive gems and the dark metal shaft… *The shaft! It's a sheath!* He grabs the scepter's orb, knowing that it's in fact not the top of a scepter, but the hilt of a sword. Holding the shaft, he yanks the hilt free and a midnight black blade slides smoothly from its metal skin. *Wow! Now that's a knife!* Not caring for the blood dripping from his palm, due to the jagged jewels within the hilt's grip, Dunlop drops the sheath and raises the blade. Donning a victorious smile, Dunlop flips a hidden switch deep within his Id and barks a gregarious, "FUCK YES!"

Spinning wildly, he looks for someone who's either seen or heard his outlandish outburst, but is quickly calmed upon the realization that he's still the only guy in the back storeroom.

Feeling like a kid next to a broken cookie jar, Dunlop hops out of the crate faster than he fell in. Once he lands on his feet, he does a double-take of his surroundings to reacquaint himself with where he is and where he needs to go. Locating the backdoor, Dunlop limps along, profusely perspiring, while cradling the scepter under his dress jacket, like Igor smuggling a brain in a jar from the lab. Due more to the humid heat of the cramped quarters, than his taxed mind and body, Dunlop is seemingly unaware that his suit is sweat-soaked through. Fixated on what lies ahead of him, versus what lies upon him or behind him, Dunlop begins to pick up the pace as a small sinister smile cracks his face.

The door at which he abruptly arrives represents a new chapter in his atrophied autobiography. Even with nothing written, he's never harbored more enthusiasm for turning the page. A surprising calmness takes hold of him, strengthening his spine as he straightens it. Looking through the door and into his future, Dunlop stands with his back straight, chest out, and chin up, intoxicated, breathing the damp, dusty, warehouse air, as if he's on a mountaintop in a York Peppermint Patty commercial.

Standing less than ten paces from the door, empowered by a new lease on life, Dunlop commits to whatever it takes, which washes his shattered soul in a warm wave of serenity. Reinvigorated by the all or nothing nature of his final destination, he resumes his departure determined, when a large man steps in front of the massive metal door with the half-lit exit sign above it, cutting off his escape five paces from freedom. Impeding his path, the man is so large that he partially obscures the view of the bottom of the exit sign. Donning a well-made, but poorly tailored suit, the man looks like he's eaten more than his fair share, while his gaudy gold chain and watch tell a tale of a man who could care less for who flipped the bill for the food.

Quickly, but casually extending his left outstretched hand to Dunlop's shoulder, he takes a firm grip, while brushing aside Dunlop's coat with the other. As the move exposes the scepter, and subsequently Dunlop's poorly planned escape plan, both men can't help but to be drawn to the room's brightest light.

Standing in front of the door like a former left tackle in front of his QB, Louie the Leopard was by far the largest piece of meat in the market. Too tough for most tastes, Louie was far from lean. Meaner than large, at 6' 8" and topping four hundred pounds, Louie the Leopard would have been more aptly named, Large Louie. His nickname had nothing to do with his agility or grace, of course, for he lacked a semblance of both. Rather, it stemmed from the seemingly random and unprovoked acts of violence he committed against unsuspecting victims, like a large cat pouncing on a baby mole. Quick and deadly, Louie went for the kill every time. He didn't scratch or bite like a cat either, but rather punched with ham hock hands. His punches were by most accounts, life-altering events, which Dunlop could appreciate as he felt the weight of Louie's left resting upon his decimated shoulder.

Always looking like he was chewing on something, conveyed a perception of philosophical credence to his questions that wasn't warranted, for in reality, Louie didn't think much at all of why he said or did things, let alone the consequences that followed. "What we got here?"

Retreating a step, Dunlop wraps around the scepter like an octopus, and hisses, "This is sanctioned."

"Sanctioned?" Louie repeats perplexed. "I run this port, and I don't remember sanctioning anything, but Catholicism. You must be here to pay tribute."

Whiffing sarcasm like a fart in church, Dunlop's sneer, masks his fear, "I'm leaving actually. I already paid at the door."

Seemingly unaware of Dunlop's disdain for his last-second shakedown, Louie opines, "That's the thing around here… You pay at the front and back. We double-bill, like the utility company." Smirking at his analogy, Louie adds, "It's an industry thing."

"I'll write you an I.O.U." Dunlop counters somewhat cantankerously.

"You a writa? You look like a writa."

"I'm a professor," Dunlop deadpans.

"Yeah, well I'm a financial advisor," Louie decrees, adding, "And right now I'd like to offer you some free advice," as he tethers Dunlop in place by squeezing tightly upon his shoulder.

"Pleased to meet you, but I think I'll pass. I'm late for an important date… Check with your boss—"

Flying off the handle harder than Dunlop had earlier, Louie's voice gets guttural, "You telling me what to do? You little prick! I'm the boss!"

Trembling from anger, not fear, Dunlop's voice becomes surprisingly steady, "No, you're a low-level thug, which is why you're watching the back door, instead of your tongue."

Enraged, Louie's voice darkens along with Dunlop's outlook, "You've made a poor decision."

Dunlop jolts backwards with startling speed and strength, freeing himself from the giant's grasp. Before Louie can fully assess his opponent's athletic attributes, Dunlop whips out the scepter and drives it into Louie's throat with both hands. Fast and furious, the attack leaves Louie only enough time to move his eyes. Transfixed upon the gleaming handle, Louie has only seconds longer before he bleeds out, switching his stare to Dunlop. His expression switches from startled to panicked as his Aorta pumps blood like a busted lawn sprinkler onto Dunlop's person. Registering the results, Dunlop yanks the scepter from Louie's esophagus and steps back far enough to allow Louie's free fall.

As Louie falls to his knees, before his final resting stop upon his face, Dunlop dismisses his diatribe, "I've made several today, but that wasn't one of them."

With that, Louie the Leopard slams face-first onto the cement. As his life force flows from him, Dunlop's builds. Breathing deep and solid, Dunlop's fatigue is replaced with vigor and a profound purpose that hovers just beyond his comprehension. Surveying the stockroom, Dunlop scans for onlookers and a place to store his first victim. Not satisfied with the options, Dunlop decides to drag Louie behind a couple of crates in the corner. Surprised at his new-found strength, Dunlop stops halfway to the drop point to survey the battlefield. Pride fires through his blood, boiling away the remainder of fear and doubt that had saddled him as of late. Simultaneously striking down every bully who had bullied him since kindergarten with one fell swoop, cleansed him of regret and remorse, while reinvigorating him with a resolve that strengthened every fiber of his being. Suddenly realizing that the pool of blood and the subsequent trail that would follow his kill to anywhere he dragged it, Dunlop laughs openly at his naivete.

After his hardy laugh at the old Dunlop's derailed train of thought, he finds himself disinterested in the recent chain of events, and steps over the Leopard like a puddle of piss, reaching the door in seven sure-footed strides. Upon opening the big steel door like a kid opening the door to the backyard on his way to play for the day, Dunlop is met by a relatively cool summer breeze and the waning light of a hard-fought day. Soaking up the shaded sunshine with his eyes closed, as if he's about to take a walk in a park, instead of across the Bronx, Dunlop opens a sly eye. Turning to Louie, Dunlop displays a cordial smile, "You look like a man of means." With that, he lets the door go as he struts to Louie's corpse. Frisking the body, he pulls a money clip and a gaudy gold keychain with a key fob from a Cadillac. "Who says crime doesn't pay?"

Springing from his squat stance, Dunlop turns and reaches the door in seconds, ripping it open like it's a rickety screen-door on a porch, instead of two-hundred pounds of steel. Surveying the packed parking lot, Dunlop taps the auto-start button on the fob, and a brand-new, fully-loaded, XTS rumbles to life. "What's a Caddy, without a daddy?"

## Chapter 9

## Cleanup in Aisle 5

Now racing behind the long strides of The Razor, Tommy is quickly becoming unhinged by the lack of communication between him and his new partner. Tommy knows the look of a man committed to kill, as The Razor looks high and low for anything remotely connected to their quarry. "Slow down, Asshole!" Tommy yells to no avail.

As Tommy tries to hide his anxiety with annoyance, The Razor's voice explodes with anger. "You!" Pointing to a lonely dock worker, trying to look busy while he checks a text message from his cell that's halfway hidden in his front jeans pocket, "Come here!"

"He don't speak no English," a heavily accented man conveys from the other side of some boxes.

The Razor turns to his right where the large Cuban stands surrounded by several young immigrants, who are assisting the floor manager in performing a QC audit of some freshly procured produce from Paraguay. The Razor's eyes instantaneously hate him, as they bore into his chest, hungering to rip his heart from his ribcage, like a switch on a wall that's connected to the last light in the room that's keeping you from sleeping off a massive hangover. Now facing the large floor manager, The Razor's tone is venomous, "But you do..."

Committed to the confrontation, the floor manager has no choice but to continue, and he does just that; walking around the boxes, he nods to his employees to stand down. They gladly acquiesce to his station, pacing their retreat step for step with his advancement towards The Razor. When he's face to face with The Razor, the true girth of the Cuban can be put into context. The same height as the 6'6" Razor, the floor manager has seventy-five pounds of solid muscle on The Razor, which he's kept in fighting shape since adding it to his seventeen-year-old emaciated frame, which had barely survived the journey to America in an innertube. Delving deep into The Razor's eyes tells him all he needs to know, for he's knocked on death's door before, and knows today won't be a ring and run. He subconsciously soothes his self-doubts by absently touching the two tattooed teardrops on his left cheek. The tattoos cheer for their champion, reminding the cautious Cuban that he's got the combat chops to survive another day. "Enough to tell you to go fuck yourself."

Tightly gripping his weapon of choice with a bent wrist, The Razor conceals the eighteen-inch blade with brass knuckles up behind his left forearm. Even though The Razor's stance hides the weapon well, it isn't the Cuban's first rodeo, and he'd known The Razor was carrying well before he stepped around the crates.

Of course, knowing is only half the battle, and what The Razor lacked in size, he more than made up for in speed. Feigning a strike from the hidden hand, which had been occupying the Cuban's countermeasure plans, he rams an open-palmed right square on the Cuban's nose. As expected, when the nose goes in, the tears come out. Stunned for a split-second, the floor manager swings a wild left to seize something that's no longer there. Predicting the lunge, The Razor has already stepped back and to the Cuban's left. Grabbing at air, trying to defend against a move he'd never see, the Cuban is undisciplined, exposing his left. The Razor sees his window and shatters it with a left windmill. The brass-armored fist incorporated into the large knife's handle, connects to the Cuban's temple with bone-jarring brutality, dropping him like a sack of spices from Somalia.

The quick, visceral victory stuns every worker to silence. In their wildest dreams, their bigger-than-life boss would never lose a fight, let alone crumble in seconds to someone half his heft. As The Razor pans his prey, his chin rises to make room for an expanding chest. He's the lion that had just leapt from the bushes onto their pack's Alpha male, dispensing with him without so much as a chip to a nail. Making sure to first freeze each man with iced eyes, he slowly lowers them to his victim. Seeing the man wasn't moving much meant The Razor could add some theatrics to his show. Casually strolling to a crate in the corner, The Razor stops to pick his huge hat off the ground, meticulously dusting it off before setting it upon his head and flicking the brim. When he arrives at the crate, The Razor takes a half-full plastic water bottle from the top and looks out among his attentive audience. "Anyone's?" Not a peep, which was not a surprise, since everyone is still standing in shocked silence. The Razor takes the silence for an answer, acquiring the agua and strutting back to his opponent, spraying him in the face. Emptying the contents of the container on the Cuban, The Razor tosses the bottle to the side, where it clatters across the floor, until settling under a wooden skid.

The floor manager, already waking from his catnap, attempts to spring to his feet as the water floods him with old memories of waves crashing upon his half-dead body, as it drifted aimlessly in the Gulf of Mexico. Though sprung into action by the spring water, the Cuban can't complete the feat, due to wobbly legs and blurred vision. Not making it past the praying position, the Cuban kneels unsteadily as he attempts to blink away cobwebs, while blood continues to gush down his face, mixing with snot, sweat and tears.

The Razor begins to strut around the floor manager, looking to the workers as he speaks, "Apologies for the rude awakening, but you passed out, and I needed to revive you in order to ask you some questions." By the time he finishes his sentence, he's standing behind the kneeling Cuban. Grabbing his thick, nappy hair with his right hand, he holds up his massive blade above his own head in the left.

"For the love of God! Stop it!" Tommy screams.

The Razor doesn't look up when he speaks to Tommy, "I need to know some things and this gentleman is not only proficient in English, but appears to be in a position of management, meaning he'll know the goings on around here. Isn't that right, Sir?"

Beaten physically, but not emotionally, the Cuban holds firm, defying The Razor, spitting before he answers, "I don't know nothing."

The Razor shows no outward reaction due to his defiance, until he rams his knife into the back of the Cuban's neck. The blade protrudes out the other side, and the Cuban does his part in the act's finale by gargling blood and spazzing his body as if The Razor had jammed an extension cord into his neck, rather than a knife.

"Holy fuck!" Tommy screeches.

Yanking his knife out with a hard pull and a boot to the back for leverage, the knife's serration makes a puddle a pool. "In lieu of that double negative, I retract 'proficient' for 'adequate'."

More shocked at The Razor's cavalier conversational quip than the actual kill, Tommy is in full panic mode, "What the fuck, Jimmy?!"

The Razor turns to Tommy, "No one calls me by my first name."

"Fucking Christ!" Tommy responds.

"Better," The Razor banters with a wink and a smile. "Now, who else doesn't know anything?" The Razor bellows as he walks from the carcass, raising his knife once again.

"Oh my God..." Tommy utters.

Taking his knife from pointing it in the air to aiming it at a young man off to his right, The Razor addresses him cordially, "Would you answer two simple questions if your life depended on it?"

"Yes," the petrified Puerto Rican answers.

"Fabulous. Have you seen a man walk through here recently who didn't belong?"

"Yes."

"Would you be so kind as to tell me where he went?"

As the warehouse worker points to the back, he keeps his eyes trained on The Razor's blade, "That way."

With the grace of an English gentleman, The Razor tips his hat, "Thank you kindly."

After his formal showing of appreciation for the worker's assistance, The Razor begins to walk in the direction of the finger without further ado. Tommy watches The Razor walk away, and begins to tremble as the enormity of the situation settles in.

Turning to the dead floor manager, lying face down in a pool of his own blood, Tommy cannot help himself, "Christ almighty! He's crazy!"

The Razor stops in his tracks. Still holding the huge knife by his side, The Razor pulls out an old timepiece from an inside pocket of his jacket and examines it. Without looking back to Tommy, he addresses him, "Tommy, be a dear and wait in the car."

"Fuck you!" Tommy yells back.

Still focused forward, The Razor reasons with Tommy. "We're going to need to make a speedy getaway when I emerge, and I'm sure you wouldn't want me in a position where I'm forced to hail a cab." Without waiting for a reply, The Razor begins his brisk walk to the back.

Tommy watches The Razor until he's hidden by a wall of boxes. Staggering backwards, Tommy misses a step as he steps on the emptied water bottle. Seeing the bottle jogs his memory. *The floor manager! For Christ's sake!* Tommy looks at the dead man one more time, absorbing every droplet of blood, before taking in his entire staff one by one. *How many people saw this? Who's gonna rat me out?* None move as Tommy sizes up the shit he's in. Tommy knows they won't move, or even utter a word before he walks out the door. He also knows if one of them calls the cops while he's waiting outside for The Razor, they'll be storming the warehouse, before they have a chance to flee.

But as the reality of the situation begins to sink in, it becomes painfully apparent that the Families will know about this regardless of when he leaves, and who he leaves alive. Even if he kills everyone in the room, someone will say something. Someone always does… And that's when it hits him like a Razor right hook; someone saw this coming and was smart enough to leave the room before the show started. As the short-lived silence of the eye-of-the-shitstorm subsides, Tommy surmises that the Families had been notified of his presence when he parked the car, so who saw what, wasn't worth worrying about. What he needed to concern himself with, was what he could control, and if he was in fact a dead man walking, he might as well be a dead man driving. Fixing his sport jacket, he buttons the top with the same thumb and index finger he just used to wipe the tears from his eyes. Looking into an imaginary mirror, Tommy nods approval at the character he's created from memories of the morning, before turning for the exit and walking to the car.

# Chapter 10

# Doubling Down

Just as the powerful late afternoon sun bakes the hard, faded, black plastic interior to the point of petrol fumes wafting off the dash, the unanswered burning questions create an atmosphere that's rapidly reaching its boiling point.

"What the fuck is going on in there?" a perturbed Putin ponders.

"Relax, Chulo. Nothing's happening in there."

"I thought The Razor was a stone-cold killer?" Putin questions.

Considering his comment, Vassy waivers, "You're right. Maybe we should go in."

Not satisfied, Putin pushes the point, "We need to call for backup is what we need to do. We're crazy. This is crazy! What were we thinking?"

"We're thinking about our careers, retirement, families, and fortunes," Vassy vocalizes.

"We're greedy," Putin counters.

"We're opportunistic, motivated, and lucky," Vassy steadfastly states.

"We're crazy," Putin adds.

As Putin trails off, Tommy hustles out, looking in every direction but in front of him.

"Tommy Two Touch… I knew I knew him," Vassy smirks.

"Thomas Tibarone the Third," Putin proclaims.

"You know him?" Vassy asks.

"Well... technically we were childhood BFF's."

"Big fucking faggots?" Vassy jokes, but Putin doesn't react.

"We were tighter than an Asian school girl..."

"What happened?" Vassy inquires.

"What happened?" Looking around the car with his hands, "This happened. I became the law and he became the outlaw."

"So?"

"So?" Putin exclaims emphatically.

"So, you can't keep your personal and business lives separate?" Vassy asks.

"It was a long time ago. We've all changed. I've seen too much to turn a blind eye to his business dealings."

"Yeah, well it looks like your boy has seen a ghost."

"That's not good. Tommy's seen a lot."

"What's happened, happened. We stay put," Vassy decrees.

"If the Professor is dead, it's on your hands," Putin viciously voices.

"Yours too, Muchacho," Vassy counters. "Besides, if he's dead, we'll have the treasure and Murder One on The Razor."

Putin ponders their play's potential, "Not a bad day's catch..."

# Chapter 11

# Listen or Go Deaf

The Razor now walks unimpeded throughout the warehouse looking for his prizes to no avail. With every step, he becomes more enraged, though to the naked eye, he looks unperturbed, as if he's speed-walking in a park merely for cardio exercise. Word travels fast throughout the warehouse of The Razor's dirty deed, and thus empties quickly, growing graveyard-silent in seconds. The Razor's hard-soled dress shoes tap loudly on the cold, damp, cement floor, echoing against the high steel walls. A truck's reverse alarm beeps somewhere in the distance. Though never stepping foot in the place, nor knowing who was involved in the transaction, The Razor knows that all shady deals end in the back, and therefore, makes a beeline to the back exit, for some much-anticipated answers.

Arriving at the backdoor, The Razor quickly scans the scene, taking in minute details that will escape the forensic team that would eventually tape the place off to investigate the murder. The Razor smells the blood before he sees it, and knows the body that the trail of blood led to was dead before it hit the ground. The brutal slaying seems to give The Razor pause. Is it respect he feels? Who could kill with such malice and then display utter indifference thereafter?

"He's gone," Edgar affirms from afar.

The Razor spins slowly on his heel, tilting his head slightly, somewhat astounded that he'd let his attention drift so thoroughly, that he'd allowed someone to sneak up on him.

Closing the distance with caution, Edgar spreads his hands to encompass the carnage, "You can walk out of here, and I won't tell the Families who was responsible for this."

Smiling at the use of such feigned bravado, "My secret's safe with you?" The Razor inquires.

As if The Razor had just whipped out a shotgun and declared war, Edgar stops dead in his tracks and assumes a defensive position, resting his hand behind his waist, hidden from The Razor. "Don't try me. I know who you are, and you don't scare me."

Laughing softly to a line he's heard bellowed before, "I scare everyone, including myself from time to time…" Looking through Edgar's soft middle to whatever weapon he was concealing that he surely hadn't mastered wielding, The Razor's smile broadens as he steps towards Edgar. "Life's tragedy is that we get old too soon and wise too late."

As The Razor closes in, Edgar cocks his stance and brandishes a crowbar over his shoulder. Looking like he's about to swat a fly with a rolled-up newspaper, The Razor is unfazed. Quickly closing the remainder of the distance, he snatches Edgar's descending arm well before the crowbar makes contact with his head. Simultaneously spinning and squatting enables The Razor to effortlessly transition Edgar's inertia over his slumping shoulder. As Edgar's frame flows forward, The Razor unsheathes his blade. By the time Edgar completes his somersault and painful landing, The Razor is behind him with the blade to the side of his head, while his other hand binds Edgar's arm behind his back. Positioned on his butt, with his legs splayed wide, Edgar has zero leverage and even fewer options. Pain pulsates throughout his body, and being that he'd taken the brunt of the fall on his tailbone, everything below his waist is unresponsive. In addition, the arm that's pinned to his spine is hot and numb at both the shoulder and wrist. Making matters worse, he's not sure if it was the landing itself, or the realization of the predicament that he's landed in that has him short of breath.

As The Razor moves close enough to nip Edgar on the nape of his neck, he muses, "Churchill once said, 'We make a living by what we get, but we make a life by what we give.'" With that, he lops off Edgar's right ear. Edgar lets out a guttural shriek that causes pigeons to scatter from the roof. Showing the indifference to Edgar's cry of a father removing a splinter from a child's palm, The Razor moves his knife to the other side of Edgar's head and announces ominously, "Now, you're going to tell me what I want to hear, or you'll never hear again."

# Chapter 12

# The Hunt Begins

Tommy's fist pounding on the steering wheel is the bass to his heartbeat's treble. The song is an erratic, tumultuous tale that has taken a decidedly disastrous direction. The Razor has gone off the reservation, and has no plans to return home until all the settlers have been scalped.

Tommy knows if he survives this day, which he most likely won't, he'll be a wanted man. Not only will the law want him in connection with the death of the innocent warehouse worker, but even more frighteningly, the other Families will want him for just showing up to the warehouse. He'd need to get out of town at a minimum, until the dust settled—maybe change his identity and make the big move.

*Cynthia! My love... my kids... Christ!* Tommy thinks next steps, and plays the end-games in rapid succession, becoming more panicked, the more he weighs his options and their eventual outcomes. *Should I call, or text the order to evacuate the Bronx and head to the safe house in New Hampshire? If The Razor lives out the day, they'll be dead by dawn. I should have them go abroad...* But then Tommy quickly reasons that the paper trail, which would include their plane tickets, hotel stays, and money conversions, would be a blazing beacon for any sleuth worth half his weight in pennies. "Son of a bitch!" Tommy screams as he rips the visor off its hinge, ushering in his own official unhinging.

The passenger side door opens, and The Razor slithers in like he's snatching the best seat in the house, while only paying for a nosebleed. "To Pelham Park, my good man, and fly like the wind!"

Tommy pulls his gun and jams it against The Razor's temple, "Fuck you! Fuck you! You crazy fucking bastard!"

The Razor, with his head pressed against a car window by a 45 Magnum, remains surprisingly calm. "Tommy, they're coming. They're coming to get us. We need to leave. Complete our—"

"Shut the fuck up, you crazy psycho fuck!"

"And they say I have interpersonal issues…"

"You killed an innocent man back there! He didn't deserve to die! You're a murdering bastard!"

"Yes."

"Yes? That's it? Yes!?"

"Yes to everything you said. I'm crazy, I'm a killer; that man was innocent, and I'm technically a bastard."

"I should kill you now. End this."

"You should drive out of here and let me end this. There's nowhere to turn now. The only one who can save you is Ellie, and if we don't complete our mission, you're useless to him. He was already on the fence about you and what you've done, or should I say, failed to do. Failure is no longer an option for either of us."

"Fuck you."

"Put the gun down. Start acting like a professional."

"A professional? You have some nerve, Pal." Tommy slowly pulls the gun from The Razor's temple, then quickly sheathes it into a concealed chest harness.

The Razor breathes a sigh of relief, the only hint he's given of being human since Tommy picked him up, "Good… I'm glad you came back. I was worried I'd have to kill you. Now let's ride."

"We got a tail."

Casually gazing into his side mirror, The Razor's eyes focus a hundred yards down the street. Squinting due to the reflection of the late afternoon sun, The Razor crinkles his long, hooked nose as if smelling what he's seeing, "So, they were there for us..."

Flabbergasted, Tommy has trouble articulating his astonishment, "Wait... What? You knew they were there... when we got here?"

"The pigs? Of course."

"And you didn't say nothing?" Tommy blurts.

"I'm just as shocked that you didn't see them, as you are that I didn't point out the obvious. Are you sure you're a criminal?" The Razor chides.

"We're dead! We're fucking dead!"

"Relax. We're fine."

"We're fine? We're fucked!"

"I need you to compose yourself and drive."

"What if I don't want to compose myself?"

"Need I remind you that if I have to drive, you have to die."

Tommy, resigning himself to the fates, slams the car in drive and locks his leg.

+ + +

"And the chase begins," Vassy prophetically proclaims.

## Chapter 12.5

Almost on the heels of the tail leaving in pursuit of Tommy and The Razor, a late-model white Lincoln Navigator and a brand new black Mercedes S Class race into the parking lot. Each vehicle emits a short chirp as the brakes clamp down hard. Even before the engines have a chance to idle, all eight doors fly open and eight men exit the large-rimmed and tinted glassed vehicles. They immediately form a semi-circle in front of the cars with a heavy-set man in his late fifties pointing orders to the warehouse behind him. Once he's done administering his hastily conceived and conveyed warehouse war plan, he claps his hands loudly, signaling the mission's beginning.

Once turned towards their target, all eight men draw their firearms, and begin an orchestrated advance. Several of them cock their guns, while one overly-ambitious henchman even goes as far as to raise his and toggle his sites between the open windows of the warehouse.

The eight men sweep the facility quickly, arriving at the bodies sooner than later. Several workers come out of the shadows, most rambling in incoherent tongues.

"How many?" the older man in the finely tailored jumpsuit demands.

"Three," Kenny Kitchens answers.

"Who?"

"Edgar, Louie, and Jesus."

"Who's Jesus?"

"The big Cuban."

"Huh?"

"The floor manager."

"Was he made?"

"No, but he was loved…"

"Fine. One from our Family, two from yours. The Catanzanos are history. Why?"

Another man speaks up, thin and young, he looks spooked by the bodies, "There was a deal that went down."

"More like went south," another Wise Guy chimes in.

"Silence!" the older man scolds. "Good men died today. Family men. Protected men."

"Sorry boss…" the Wise Guy relents.

"What deal?" The older man inquires.

"Some kind of valuable art… artifact maybe… from South America," the kid conveys.

"Where?" the older man asks.

"Pelham Park?" the kid offers as a possibility.

"Pelham Park… Fine. It's our only lead. I want a dozen of my guys there now." Looking to Kenny Kitchens, "How many your Family gonna send?"

"We'll send a dozen as well. And I'll go there personally to ensure justice is served," Kenny Kitchens states with a clenched jaw.

"Very well. Remember, Gentlemen, this is a business trip. These men died, and we need to make sure their families are taken care of. Their life insurance policy is in Pelham Park. Make sure you don't leave without their premiums."

## Chapter 13

## Pro Ho on the Go

Like a nineteen-year-old arriving in South Beach for spring break, Dunlop is anxiously awaiting his first sexual escapade in what feels like forever and a day, "And I thought Hunts Point was a meat market!" Dunlop dishes aloud to no one.

Surveying the selection, Dunlop begins to pull wood. Strong, hard wood, like aged oak. Dunlop feels the warm embrace of the vim and vigor that had left him at the altar more than two decades ago. Finally anticipating what will happen next, rather than dreading it, produces a Mad Libs' shit-eatin' grin. The hookers come in all shapes and sizes: tall, lanky Russians, to voluptuous ebony hourglasses that look sturdy enough to withstand a Mike Tyson fist fucking.

Not looking to touch skin whiter than his own, he passes on the Eastern Bloc bitches, while conceding his cock may not even scrape a sidewall of one of the cavernous colored clitorises. Looking to strike a sexy mix of size and shade, his eyes are drawn down the block to the rearview of a five-foot, three-inch, creamy Cuban that's currently poured into a short yellow spandex dress. Having the agility of a Cirque du Soleil hire wire act, allows her to sway her hips in six-inch stilettoes to an old Tribe Called Quest remix emanating from a barbershop three stores down.

An impulse purchase for the ages that would surely eclipse the Fruit Ninja blender he purchased for his uncle who wouldn't eat anything that wasn't fried, Dunlop knows the fantasy is not only fleeting, but frivolous. It's the thought that counts that has him hit the gas. The Caddy effortlessly accelerates to the end of the block, and thus, Dunlop almost passes her, before he must slam on the brakes to hold even. Her face is full, but not fat. Her hair is blacker than his thoughts, while her lips are so big, they looked to be pilfered off the Hawaiian Punch pitcher. Hoping she can quench his thirst with an enthusiastic, "Oh, yeah!", Dunlop drops a devilish, "Pardon, Miss…" As if Dunlop had whispered it with the windows up, the hooker pays him no heed, and continues on her way, swaying seductively to the sounds of the street. Somewhat flustered, Dunlop's voice raises, "Miss?!"

Though the hooker continues on her way, Dunlop notices her head twitch ever so slightly, as she registers the remark. Dunlop is beyond beside himself. Horny and happy were thrown to the curb by annoyed and astonished. If he were to be rejected now by a woman who literally got paid to fuck, he couldn't live with himself, nor allow her to live. *Who the fuck does she think she is? I'm the best thing that's ever happened to this stupid bitch!*

Dunlop brings the car within inches of the hooker, "Excuse me, Miss, would you happen to know where I can get my cock sucked around here?"

The hooker stops on a dime, as if Dunlop had yelled a warning that the next piece of pavement had a hidden boobytrap, rather than he wanted her boobies.

The hooker's voice is angry and oddly afraid, "You out yo mind, Chulo?"

Dunlop is miffed, "I'm not sure what a 'chulo' is… Wait, did you just call me an ice cream taco?"

"Huh?" the hooker responds with a furrowed brow.

Frustrated, Dunlop exhales to collect his thoughts, not looking to beat around the bush, but not looking to lose it either, "Look, my cock is about to explode and I'd prefer that to happen in one of your orifices." Knowing as it left his mouth, it would mean he'd have a better chance of being blown by himself than the hooker, he closes his eyes to await his comeuppance.

"Fuck off, Pig!" the hooker yells.

Taken aback, Dunlop grins, "Oh, you think I'm a cop?"

His face goes from grin to grim when the hooker sets him straight, "No. I think you're a pig. Fuck off!"

Reverting back to the old, desperate Dunlop, he begins to grovel, "I'm sorry. I'm just horny and nervous. Please, I'll play nice and finish quick… Heck, I'll even over pay."

As Dunlop remains frozen with a nervous smile, the hooker lays it out, "You ain't cumming in me, unless you're wearing a jimmy…"

"Fair enough," Dunlop amiably agrees.

The Hooker thinks about it, rolls her eyes and then walks over and hops in Dunlop's car.

Flicking down the vanity mirror of the car, the hooker whips out hot pink lipstick. "If you want the money shot, it's $50 extra. So is kissing skin."

"Fantastic," Dunlop asseverates as he switches pedals and accelerates up to a quick cruising speed. "Not to brag, but I probably have the cleanest cock you've ever sucked. I'm OCD."

The hooker grabs the door and tries to open it.

Caught off guard by the erratic behavior of his passenger, Dunlop half-stops as he swerves, attempting to grab her, while checking the door locks, "Hey!"

"Fuck you! I'm not going to jail Pig! Nothing happened! Let me da fuck out a heeer!"

"What? Oh, no... OCD is a condition, not a position."

"Can I catch it?"

"No."

"So OCD ain't no agency, and we ain't on our way downtown so you can book me?"

Dunlop unzips his pants and whips out his dick, "I'll tell you what, why don't you go down on this, while I drive us to the park for some beautiful love making."

Putting her lipstick away in her cleavage, the hooker flutters her lashes, "Please... if you want to fuck outside, that's an additional $50."

Flabbergasted, Dunlop runs his hand through his disheveled hair, "You got more hidden fees than a credit card company."

"A. I don't take credit cards. And, B. they ain't hidden, 'cause I'm telling you straight up."

Looking in his lap, "Speaking of straight up, I think he's ready."

Setting her sights on the job at hand, the hooker giggles, "Make love? You trippin..."

Swallowing him whole before she finishes her sentence, Dunlop's smile is broad, as he relaxes into the thirty-way adjustable seat.

Looking at her outstretched, barely clothed body as she goes about her business, Dunlop steals a stare into the rearview mirror, offering himself a whimsical wink of approval, before offering himself already heeded advice. "If you're going to wait your whole life to arrive, do it in style."

# Chapter 14

# Criminal Commitment

When you're waiting, time slows. When you're anxious, time hurts. When you're against the clock, time is your enemy. Cold and unbending, time is a continual force with no equal, no conscience, and thus, no mercy. Currently, time was gobbling up the dynamic duo's carefully laid plans, faster than Putin had gobbled up the hero from Mario's. But unlike Putin, time couldn't be satiated. Never satisfied, never appeased, time continues in its unending quest to outlast everything. Trailing Tommy Two Touch and the hitman from a safe distance was an arduous endeavor at best; trying to arrive at an unknown rendezvous point before them, was mission impossible.

At his wit's end, Vassy sighs, "They're taking their sweet ass time."

Putin looks in his side-mirror for a tail that would never materialize, "Their plan is to take care of all the loose ends at once, and that's gonna be at the drop zone."

Not taking his eyes from the road, Vassy remains unconvinced of Putin's prediction, "Risk it in public? Please…"

"This meeting is happening in public, but not in plain sight."

Vassy squints more than he should for a guy supposedly sporting 20/20 vision on a perfectly lit, dusk drive. "A Benjamin says they whack him before he makes it to the drop box."

"I'll take your action, Paco, but let's clarify: dollars, not pesos."

Puckering at the slight, Vassy agrees, "You're on, Mighty Cong."

Putin addresses the question on Vassy's lips, "They're going to want to see who the contact is, and obviously take his money."

Shaking his head at a wrong answer, Vassy emphatically states his case, "You don't get the M.O. of The Razor. There isn't a multi-staged retribution and post-fuck up financial fixer-up model that he's going to enact."

Putin nods with his lips pressed hard, acknowledging his partner's insight, but it's his turn to enlighten, "I might not get your Razor, but I get Tommy."

"That won't stop The Razor," Vassy fires back.

"Tommy isn't here to stop him; he's here to follow Catanzano's orders to a tee. Catanzano may want the Professor dead, but he also wants his money and treasure, and whatever the fuck else he can get his greedy mob hands on."

"I'm sure he wants all of it, including the Professor's balls on a sub with provolone, but the Razor could care less."

Putin looks to his partner, "You think he'll defy a direct order from Catanzano?"

Tense from tailing, Vassy's snaps a response, "For the last time, The Razor answers to no one. Catanzano will be hopeful that he brings back everything, but in the end, he knows he'll get what he's paid for... Crazy."

Putin ponders the play, "So The Razor can't help himself?"

"Like a shark at a feeding frenzy. He'll smell blood and go for the kill. Fill his belly, and leave."

Dissecting the picture his partner painted, Putin prophesizes, "With that said, I think the likelihood of him waiting until the drop is even greater."

Stumped by Putin's staggering stupidity, Vassy exhales, "Why?"

Putin portentously proclaims, "If not to take the money from the buyer, then to take his life… Send a message to even more people. You know, kill two birds with one stone."

As the significance of the statement settles in, Vassy cannot help but be impressed, "I can't believe I'm saying this, but I follow your logic."

Putin smiles, "He won't even notice us. You know that, right?"

"I hate to say this, but we'll have to take your boy out first."

"Easier said than done. Besides, I may be able to convince him to do the right thing for once."

"You trust him?"

"I'm not sure I trust myself…"

"Don't get flighty on me now, Partner," Vassy scolds.

"Tommy didn't think this through. He's not a thinker. He's a doer. He'll do what's right."

"I bet he never thought he'd ever be the second most dangerous guy on the job."

"They don't call him Two Touch, because he pulls punches," Putin pontificates.

# Chapter 15

# Joy Riding

As Dunlop takes in the sights, sounds, and smells of the streets, he's warmly reminded why this drive is better than any he's made in recent memory, as a blast of warm, wet air wafts through the open windows from a Cuban restaurant on the corner, engulfing his nasal passages with heavily spiced, roasted pork. For starters, his broken-down Civic with fewer options than a prison breakfast menu, and more city miles than the hooker currently blowing him, could never transport him in such luxury. And secondly, he couldn't remember taking such a meaningful drive since the birth of his first child. Though the XTS was palatial compared to his current car, after this deal he'd get himself a proper luxury car befitting someone of his station. *Maybe I'll get a Bentley for when I want to drive, and a Rolls for when I want to be driven?* Grinning from the satisfaction of knowing he'd become tired of the jarring ride of an Italian sports car, while his understated elegant persona would be chapfallen with the brash and trash lifestyle that centered around such extroverted boy toys.

He knew himself well, and was ecstatic that he'd finally come out of his shell. He fancied himself a smart, savvy, sophisticated, sensible man. Considering today was his rebirth, the irony wasn't lost on him that he was properly seasoned, as well. His soul was also older today somehow than it was yesterday. His internal growth and self-actualization meant he no longer considered himself merely a professor, nor did the antiquated social status of father and husband sound as meaningful as once before. He could be whatever he wanted to be and what he'd been in the past were just points in his existence that had trained him for today—bullet points on his life's resume. Living life to its fullest was his manifest destiny.

He begins to wonder whether he's even enjoying driving the car, since he most likely should be chauffeured to his public appearances and business meetings, while emaciated runway models double team him in the backseat at the very minimum. Looking down at the soloist performing her opus, he ponders if she's even worthy of his wiener. *Does she even deserve my dick? I had to ask her? Her?! No, she made me beg! Didn't she? Fucking Mexican street food...She'll pay for that... Disrespecting me was her last mistake. Actually, her last mistake is this subpar suck job she's fronting as fellatio.*

As Dunlop muses his date's fate, he hardly notices the commotion on the corner created by his car. Apparently the 4th Street Latinos know his former car's owner, and when one of the gang members looks inside the car and doesn't see Louie, but Dunlop, he can't help but follow the form down to the hooker going down on him.

Tapping the huge Latino next to him with the outside of his arm, the wiry, tattooed, Latino is in a jovial mood, "Yo, Papi! Check it... Anita is working overtime."

All three hundred pounds of the white tank top-donned gang leader turns to look inside the stationary car. Smiling, the gang leader addresses Dunlop, "Hey Gringo, looks like good times. Huh?"

The gang leader's voice snaps Dunlop from his tribulations. Annoyed at both his flawed relationship with the hooker, and her flawed fellatio, Dunlop is cheeky with his response, "You jealous?"

Sensing something afoot other than a grateful client, the gang leader loses his smile, almost as fast as he finds his hand on his back-pocket that conceals his Glock, "What if I am?"

Smirking at the setup, Dunlop can't help but diss him, "You can blow me next."

Timing the insult with the green light, Dunlop hits the gas and sticks his finger out the window, leaving the gang with his vapor trail and a hurled insult of, "Fucking Beaners!"

The hooker raises her head for a much-needed gasp of air, inquiring, "What's a beaner?"

Temporarily forgetting his newfound fuck friend was even in the front seat, let alone fluffing his frank, Dunlop finds himself somewhat embarrassed by his social faux pas, "Oh... that's the band, The Beaners... I think they're a Mariachi band..." Readjusting himself in the seat, he waits for her brow to furrow, before redirecting her attention to the greater good, "Hey, less talky, more sucky." Pushing her head back into his lap, he cranks the tunes from the steering wheel, offering the rearview mirror a quick wink, before pressing the pedal to the metal.

## Chapter 15.33

The vehicles await their occupants with the patience of the dead. The white Lincoln Navigator and blacked out Mercedes S Class sit still with engines off and windows down. The eight angry men stand in a circle as quiet as their rides. The only sounds emitted from the group are the occasional magazines being clipped to a gun, for pros don't cock their guns until they get to the target. Double checking the strength of straps and barrels for debris, the faces scream revenge, as the posse prepares for justice.

"Lock. Load. Let's go."

## Chapter 15.66

Heading south on East Tremont Ave, the low riding, 2007, gold-speckled Dodge Charger with 24-inch rims, is packed with Puerto Ricans, and riding so close to the lead pursuit vehicle that a horsefly could bumper fuck them. The Joker purple, 1978 Cadillac Brougham with jet-black tinted windows, muscles its way through traffic with quiet confidence. Transporting four gang members, including the gang's 300-pound-plus Kingpin, Javier Cruz, aka Mr. Meat, the Brougham maintains the appropriate distance from Dunlop as to not blow, or lose, the tail. Losing Dunlop isn't an option for Mr. Meat, for he'd been insulted in front of his men, on his home turf. If he didn't restore order quickly, he'd lose entire control of his enterprise by dawn. As the light under the highway overpass turns yellow, Javier's knuckles turn white on the wheel. *What's he doing?* Dunlop turns on his right blinker and slows, looking as if he's about to pull into the parking lot of Frenchy's. Javier turns down the music in his car, and raises his hand. His right-hand man, who is literally to his right, riding shotgun, taps a text to the trailing Charger on his burner phone. The light turns red, and Dunlop does the unthinkable for someone not knowing he's being tailed; he hits the gas and blows the light.

"Shit!" Javier screams.

"Fuck, Papi! What now?"

Not looking away from the speeding XTS, Javier addresses Jorge and the other two in his car, "He ain't getting out of the Bronx alive."

"You're driving with a suspended license, Papi. You can't blow this light," Jorge chastises.

"I know where he's going," Javier hisses.

"Where?"

"To the park."

"Pelham?"

"Yeah."

"How you know he's not skipping town?"

"He would have kept heading east on Pelham if he was planning on 95," Javier states.

"Yeah, and why else would you go this way other than the water?" the sidekick concedes.

"No reason."

The sidekick texts something to a passenger in the gold-speckled Charger as Javier hits the gas at the newly greened light.

# Chapter 16

# Late for an Important Date

Picking up the pace since blowing the light, Dunlop cuts off his fair share of motorists, bicyclists, and outdoor enthusiasts who are trying to enjoy the early evening, despite the stifling humidity that has come on stronger than Dunlop's new disposition. The hooker's disposition hasn't changed since she worked her first trick at the age of fifteen, but her position has altered significantly, due to the erratic pole position pace Dunlop has maintained. No longer able to perform the task at hand, the hooker braces herself upright with her right hand gripping the door handle, while her left strangles that stalk of her seat belt. Dunlop doesn't seem to notice the absence of such skilled labor, and when he slams the car into a stall next to the bathrooms, he almost forgets she's there. Opening the door, he turns to his passenger, who is still staring straight ahead, with the unreadable expression of someone viewing the weather portion of the nightly news.

Dunlop arches an eyebrow, while he analyzes her mannequin impression. Realizing she's not in the mood for charades, he asks the obvious, "You coming?"

"Am I coming? Question is, are you cumming for a third time?" Crossing her arms, the hooker turns her head and looks out her open window.

Leaning over the armrest, Dunlop pours on the charm, "Is this our first fight?"

"Tú eres un maricón," the hooker scolds.

Tensing somewhat, Dunlop is terse in his delivery, "You know how I hate to air our dirty laundry in public like this."

"I ain't going nowhere until I get paid for what I've already done," the hooker states emphatically.

Looking around the center console and armrest for money, Dunlop appears tired for a moment, then brightens when a lightbulb flashes brilliance, "Tell ya what… I'll give you the car when we're done? Fair?"

"Fuck you!  You take me fo some dumb-ass bitch?"

"Actually, up until now, I've rather enjoyed our time together."

"Please… give me money, or I ain't yo honey!"

"So, you won't go?"

Looking Dunlop up and down with disapproval, "You deaf?  I don't get paid, you don't get laid."

Sighing, Dunlop seems to consider their options before suggesting a proper course of action, "I hate to say this, but… if you don't get out of this car right now and come with me, I'll repeatedly stab you in the stomach and leave your dead hooker snatch to bleed out, while I find another whore for the chore."

"Hel---!"

Dunlop grabs the hooker by the hair before she can escape out the passenger door.  She grabs his hand with both of hers, but before she can implement her countermeasures, Dunlop delivers a flurry of twenty-five furious thrusts of his scepter into her belly. Stopping from exhaustion with the scepter still lodged in the hooker's belly, Dunlop inhales deep to catch his breath. Looking her still form over, he rolls his eyes from the annoyance, not the agony.  Gripping his chest since it began to heave from the exhilarating workout, he notices something as it steadies to a calming rhythm. Loosening his grip, he smiles at the lump in his jacket, then pats it as he looks up to the dead hooker somewhat astonished, "Wait, what's this?" Pulling back his tweed jacket, he offers his victim a sly smile as he rams his hand into the inside pocket and yanks out Louie the Leopard's money clip. Waving it in front of the dead hooker he sheepishly admits, "Now that's uncomfortable. I'd forget my penis if it wasn't attached to my pelvis."

Realizing his highbrow humor is once again lost on his traveling companion, he exits the vehicle, straightens and flick-cleans his jacket, shakes his hair down, and walks away with the bloodied scepter by his side, in plain sight. As he quickly distances himself from the brutal slaying both physically and emotionally, he can't help but shake his head as the awe of his brilliance overpowers him once again, "Whore for the chore… I should have taught poetry."

### Chapter 16.25

The Charger and Brougham accelerate into the parking lot and make a beeline to the parked XTS. Skidding to stops on either side of the car one stall away, the quickly fleeing sun obscures the view of the passenger. The head folded forward screams dead, but it's not until the all eight men pour out of their rides and rush to the sides can the true horror scene be taken in.

Looking to his leader, the sidekick looks pale, "He got his freak on."

Javier pulls his sidekick away from the window and bends down to the window ledge level. Looking over her with an odd affection, he gently moves her head with both hands until it rests on the headrest. Fixing her blood-soaked hair, as if she's his daughter sleeping off a high fever, he whispers to his men, "Five large for who gets him to me first."

The gang members all cock their weapons in unison and begin to jog away, but stop on a dime when Javier raises his head and voice, "Alive! Do what you want to him, but make sure there's enough left of him for me, or you'll be joining him. Vámanos!" All the gangsters nod in understanding, and then jog off into the park. Some take the path, others the lawn.

The sidekick eyes his leader, "I haven't seen you this crazy since you got out the block, Papi."

Looking back at his loyal employee, Javier's jaw muscles flex as he swallows a lump of coal, "First he hurt my feelings, then he hurt my business. Now I hurt heaven…"

## Chapter 16.50

Tommy knows where to go. Two blocks away from his nest egg is the best park-access money can buy. An avid speed walker, Tommy and his wife have put their money to good use, walking the park most weekends regardless of the season. This time, Tommy is painfully aware that this isn't going to be a walk in the park. As they screech into the lot, Tommy identifies the pack of oddball automobiles at the far end, close to the bathrooms. The joker purple and gold dust mingle with the black Caddy, mimicking the colors that would adorn an island country's flag. Tommy makes a beeline to the clusterfuck of cars, and memorizes each license plate with a blink of his eyes, taking several mental snapshots. As he pieces the puzzle together from the pictures he's taken, The Razor flings the car door open and ejects himself, slamming the door behind himself, before Tommy can protest his jumpstart.

"Shit," is all Tommy can muster under his breath as he pulls his ride into a parking slot. Before exiting his ride, he takes a big breath and a slow scan of his immediate surroundings for both the gang bangers and his neighbors, who are surely walking to and fro the park at this time of night.

The Razor's long gait closes in on the cluster of cars quickly. Without any regard for who may still be lingering, or what has transpired previously that would be currently garnering attention in their direction, The Razor demonstrates zero hesitation as he approaches the passenger-side front door of Dunlop's Caddy.

As Tommy jogs over, holding his sports jacket closed, The Razor muses out loud, "Looks like our Professor Dunlop has acquired a taste…"

Tommy pulls up slightly out of breath, more so to do with the gravity of the moment, rather than the distance he's covered to witness it. "Shit… that don't fit the guy I knew."

Donning a dark, knowing smile, The Razor quips, "You may have met him on several occasions, Tommy, but you never got to truly know him."

Tommy must expend the same amount of energy to pull his stare from the dead hooker as one would expend pulling a magnet from a fridge, "The other cars look like 4th Street Latinos. I gather she's theirs?"

The Razor looks longingly at the Latino, as if she was still alive and someone he loved, "She belongs to Mr. Dunlop… now and forever."

The comment pulls Tommy's stare from the distant grassy knoll, where the parties are surely headed, back to his deeply disturbed teammate. Shaking his head in utter astonishment, "Let's go. We're late."

The Razor turns from the dead hooker to Tommy, taking his sweet-ass time to adjust the brim of his hat just so. Upon satisfaction of the hat's fit, he extends his hand, while slightly bowing his head, graciously offering Tommy the lead. Tommy reluctantly takes it, and the tandem of Tommy and Terrifying, head off into the park for an evening stroll.

## Chapter 16.75

As Putin drifts into the lot, pushing the car's capability envelope, he's acutely aware that he's going to see someone he knows sooner than later. He just hopes he sees them before they're flying over the hood of his car. If his wife catches him driving like a maniac in their backyard, he's gonna wish he'd drowned with the kid. Though driving at such a panicked pace has occupied every nerve in his system for the past fifteen minutes, he still has the ability to process the parking lot in its entirety, instantly honing in on the cars parked in the far corner, near the bathrooms.

"We've got a packed park tonight," a peevish Putin postulates.

"Shit…" Vassy mutters under his breath.

The car takes ten seconds to close the distance, and the men are out of the car, with guns drawn behind opened doors within one more. Pointing their pieces between empty cars, it takes another three seconds before they can confirm that the party has moved. Of course, they perform a quick shakedown of the rides before moving on. Putin stays put with his gun trained on the ride Vassy rolls to first—Dunlop's.

Once again, Vassy's athletic abilities do not fit the mold of someone with fat folds; sprinting the twenty feet in a blink of an eye. Putin holds steady, adjusting his aim from one open window to another, as he surveys the other cars with his peripheral vision. The purple Caddy with the blacked-out windows garners more of his attention than he wants, but the fact that it could house five guys with guns trained on them without their knowledge makes him more than a little uneasy. Even more unnerving is his seasoned partner's complete disregard for the potential kill zone that he's just blindly run into. *How did he miss it? Where's his head?* Putin knows he'll need a focused Vassy in order to leave this park alive tonight.

"Oh fuck…" Vassy stutters as he stumbles back a few uncoordinated paces.

Putin knows whatever Vassy is fixated on in the front seat of Dunlop's ride is beyond bad. Gut instincts tell Putin the coast is clear, allowing him to move from behind the door panel and stagger towards his partner with beleaguered determination. He could see her hair pouring out the window from five feet behind the car. When he positions himself alongside Vassy, the sight is earth-shattering.

"Oh my God…" is all that can escape Putin's labored breath.

While Vassy raises the clenched cross that hangs from a set of Old World rosary beads to his lips for repeated dry kisses, the other hand feverishly makes more cryptic signs than a third base coach during the final out of the World Series.

Putin doesn't look up from the hooker. "Can we call for backup now?"

Stopping his roadside service, Vassy pulls himself together, vanquishing Putin's vacillation, "We're in too deep!"

Putin's frightened face turns to Vassy, "The Razor's already gone into kill mode! Look at that poor girl... Look!" Turning back to the hooker, Putin rests his free hand on the windowsill, while his gun hangs limp in the other.

Looking away from the girl, Vassy scans the grassy knoll, the other rides, and the entrance to the park, before he addresses the obvious, "You don't know that was The Razor..."

"What? Who the fuck else would have slaughtered her—an innocent bystander?"

Shaking the crime from his cranium will never be second nature, but Vassy has mastered the art of keeping clear, by alienating fear, "We've got to move faster, that's all."

Shocked by his partner's cavalier conclusion, Putin is cancerous in his counter. "We're racing into a kill zone! Those cars belong to the 4th Street Latinos."

Nodding, Vassy adds, "Yeah, and so does the hooker."

Finally looking up to his partner, Putin asks, "You still wanna go Wild West on this? Cause I think we're slightly outgunned, Partner."

"That's fine, because we're not going in guns a'blazing. We're doing this stealth style... This just might actually work to our advantage."

Putin's eyes light up, as his mind searches for successful scenarios, "With all the confusion... my God! That's it! I can't believe I'm following your logic on this one."

Looking around the park with a jerk's smirk, Vassy inhales deeply, "Can you smell that? That's success my friend."

"Actually, it's the hoagie again. My bad."

"Disgusting! Let's move!"

# Chapter 17

# Get Ready, Get Set, Go!

The Lincoln Navigator and Mercedes S-class fly into the lot with complete disregard for public safety. The lead driver sees the car collection at the far end of the lot, and the two cars go from fast to furious. Not bothering with stalls, the cars slam-stop a safe distance from the parked cars and the men pour out of the vehicles, guns drawn. Shotguns are pumped and barrels are cocked, as the posse surrounds the abandoned vehicles. With a weapon trained on every window, two men immediately open the back doors to the blacked-out Brougham.

One of the foot soldiers who'd been unlucky enough to pull watch on Louie's car is the first to view the carnage, "For fuck's sake!"

The Lieutenant, Kenny Kitchens, demands an answer as he scampers to his side, "What?"

"Some hooker looks like she's had an Obama Care caesarian."

Kenny arrives just in time to look away before the bile in his throat opens the flood gates. Composing himself, the Lieutenant turns to the Underboss, "Looks like whoever stole Louie's ride had a close shave with The Razor."

The Underboss clearly has no interest in viewing the details. He looks around with a puss on his face before inquiring, "Who owns the other rides?"

One of the other soldiers points to Vassy and Putin's ride, "That's the Undercover's ride."

Kenny seems somewhat perplexed, "They were there for our guy, huh?"

The robust Underboss, Benny Big Band, bemoans, "He must be a real VIP. The cops, the Catanzanos, and if I'm not mistaken, those belong to the 4th Street Latinos?", pointing with his thumb over his shoulder at the gold-speckled Dodge Charger and the Joker purple '78 Caddy Brougham.

Kenny Kitchens contemplates the license plates, "Makes sense. The hooker is one of theirs."

Mickey Meathead, a made Man, who made his name the old-fashioned way inquires, "How you know?"

Apprehensively answering, Kenny looks away from the others, "Her tats…"

"When did you see her tats?" Mickey pries.

"I like Latinas, okay? I know her. She's one of theirs…"

"Sorry…" Mickey whispers.

With a loud snort, Kenny clears the air, "No tears… I wasn't planning on proposing."

Benny Big Band clearly could care less, "We split up in groups of two."

One of the soldiers shouts out, "The Latinos will be out for blood!"

Benny looks to the soldier, and silences him with a look instead of a word, since he's from the other Family, "Shoot anything that moves."

The soldier nods, but another asks, "What about The Razor?" This soldier was from Benny's Family, and knew to follow orders and not question them, "What about him?" Benny levels.

The soldier from the other Family who spoke out of turn, follows up for him, "We going to try to take him alive and bring him back like we's ordered to?"

Benny spins to the soldier, "Pardon?"

Though the soldier wasn't looking for trouble with Benny, his next comment troubles Benny and Kenny. "Both bosses made it clear they want him to squirm before he meets the Creator."

Kenny knows the inquiry is genuine, but he also knows dissension is fostered from free-will, and with two Families competing for the same prize, the competitive nature was bound to make a messy situation ugly. Turning on his soldier, he scolds, "When the fuck did you get a private audience that I wasn't privy to?"

Mickey chimes in, "He ain't eva meetin' no Creator."

The soldier's fears are clearly not assuaged by the pep talk, "That said, we're—"

Benny is at his wit's end, "The Razor's going straight to Hell. No pearly gate formalities."

The soldier knows he's got to answer to Kenny, but not Benny. "So, what's that got to do with his come-uppance while he's still here?"

Kenny doesn't like where this is going. His soldier knows it's a team play and he isn't playing nice with the others. "If you're smart, you take whatever shot you got. Don't hesitate. You see him, chances are he's already seen you."

Benny doesn't seem to notice the slight, "Kenny's right. Let us worry about the bosses. You worry about The Razor and that fucking little cocksucker that stole Louie's car and his future."

"Don't forget about Tommy Two Touch. He's an animal," one of the other soldiers states aloud.

Another soldier asks, "Why do they call him Tommy Two Touch?"

Kenny looks at his watch, then up to the sunless sky, "Put it this way… If Tommy's touching you for a third time, it's strictly for disposal purposes."

"And the cops?" The soldier follows up with.

Benny shoots in, "Yeah, them too."

"Whoa. Killing cops… I didn't sign-up for that," another soldier sounds off.

Benny smiles inwardly, "This one's on the house, Gentlemen."

"How so?" the soldier inquires.

Benny muses, "Something tells me this little excursion hasn't been cleared through headquarters."

"Why's that?" Mickey asks.

"Because," Benny levels, "If it were legit, half the department would already be here, with the other half on the way."

The soldier, not being the brightest bulb in the chandelier, can't add zeroes, let alone master advanced reasoning, "The entire Force, for a hooka?"

Exhausted by stupid men asking even dumber questions, Benny looks to the hazy evening sky for help, "No… another dead hooker wouldn't warrant a meter maid."

Kenny sees his good friend about to crack and figures he'd better speed up the process once again, "They're here for whatever Louie's killer's got."

Benny looks into the eyes of each man, before throwing down the gavel, "And make no mistake about it, so are we."

"Business is business, Gentlemen. Time to recoup our losses!" Kenny Kitchens emphatically decrees.

Benny wants to make sure everyone is on the same page, "Kill everyone. And I mean everyone. Tommy, The Razor, the bangers, the cops... You see a fucking couple on a moonlit stroll—dead. It moves, it dies... Capiche?"

Everyone's heads nod in understanding.

Kenny doesn't like the last part, but knows now is the time for doing, not debating details, "Let's go to work, Gentlemen."

Eight men simultaneously cock their weapons.

## Chapter 18

## Building Momentum

Viewing your future through a gray scale scope of self-pity and doubt will lead you lost more often than not, and Professor Dunlop has finally found himself in the middle of nowhere, with anywhere being the way out. Up to this moment, it seemed as if the world was against him, with the creator himself, foiling his manifest destiny. But now the thought of even God trying to stop him, doesn't seem quite that daunting. *God is powerful, but all powerful?? Not so sure...* Something was empowering Dunlop and though he didn't know what it was, he knew beyond a shadow of a doubt it wasn't God. Or at least he knew it wasn't the supreme being that his fellow mortals had for so long worshipped as the one true God. He was feeling quite powerful himself as of late—God-like to be more precise. *What constitutes a God? Would I still be considered a mere mortal? I feel immortal. I've always been smarter than everyone... Maybe all I was missing was the strength... The courage has always been there, though it's been suppressed for all these years by the very people I loved. Harnessing my greatness to empower themselves... Feed off of me like sponges, will you! They should be the ones feeding me! Sacrifices should be made to me! I should be fed with the souls of the undeserving! The unbelievers! Believe me, obey me, fear me... I am the true ruler of Man. I am God!*

With the pace of someone catching a train for which they're just on time, but not yet late, Dunlop's strides are fast, powerful and purposeful. He's drawn in a direction, with his destination and destiny coming into focus by the footfall. With his place within the Universe secured, humanity awaits with bated breath as he ascends to the top of the pyramid that he was so unjustly struck from, so very long ago. *They were jealous of me then, and now they're scared of my retribution. I don't blame them... Fear my wrath! Time to pay for original sin...*

"Hey, Mister!"

Dunlop hears the heavy accent from fifty paces back. Something inside screams danger. The voice seems too innocent. *Who would be trying to hail me in the middle of the night?* As Dunlop abruptly runs right, a bullet grazes his left jacket sleeve. Running behind a tree, Dunlop feels the wind and wisp from several errant bullets. The tree takes a hit. The thud jolts Dunlop. The realization that people are still trying to stop him from ruling what's rightfully his, jars bestial anger loose. He needs to get to that man, and make him pay for this insufferable act of indignation! *How dare he shoot at his Lord and savior!? Your soul will be your sacrifice. I hope for your sake, it appeases me...*

# Chapter 19

# You Are What You Eat

As Tommy and The Razor walk up to the seventh murder scene, Tommy is not only unnerved by the gunshots and screams over the past twenty minutes, but unhinged by the sickly staged sacrifices that are Dunlop's latest victims. Not himself since viewing the hooker, Tommy is traumatized by each victim they view. For with each kill, Dunlop grows more bold, more violent, more evil…more expressive? This particular kill is arranged similarly to the last one, something Dunlop had begun to develop after kill four. Discussing death via the lifeless bodies of his victims, Dunlop was telling a tale of terror and Tommy was being forced into the role of attentive audience.

Body five, a thin, ugly 4th Street Latino with a T-shirt so blood-stained it looked to have come from the factory red, was found with his shoes off. Tommy assumed that they'd been stolen by a homeless person who'd happened to be in the area when the gang banger was killed, but The Razor knew better, and when they found the red, white and blue Puma high-tops twenty feet up the path with their heels connecting on top of a puddle of piss, their worst fears were confirmed.

Kill number seven is not only gruesome for its visceral mutilation, but for its message. Not only had the man been bludgeoned by the blunt end of the scepter, after he was clearly killed by repeated stab wounds to his chest, but his fist had been lodged in his mouth. His cheeks were sliced from the sides of his lips towards his ears and his teeth looked to either have been kicked in, or more likely, bashed in with the scepter's handle, to make room for his fist.

"Holy fucking Christ, O fucking mighty!" Tommy yelps.

"I'm glad I'm not the only who appreciates a job well done."

"Well done? You sick fucking bastard! That's Mickey "Meathead". We played little league together at St. Pat's…"

"St. Pat's… You love sports Tommy. I love the Arts, and this is a masterpiece."

Flabbergasted, Tommy stares at The Razor with eyes wide, "Masterpiece? You think this is beautiful?!"

The Razor reexamines the scene of the crime once more before he orates, "It is not sufficient to see and to know the beauty of a work. We must feel and be affected by it."

Shaking his head, Tommy looks away from The Razor, and back to his old friend, "That's revolting."

"No, that's Voltaire," The Razor counters.

Lost for some time in the fog of war, Tommy's patience is frayed, "Vol who? You and your French bullshit!"

The Razor is in deep thought and pays Tommy's lack of curiosity no mind, "I wonder what he said or did, or what he represented to the Professor, for him to position him in such a way…"

"Does it matter? He's blowing his fist for Christ's sake!"

Still ignoring Tommy's outbursts, as if he's his son, bored at an art museum, The Razor muses, "Or is he just eating his own words... Maybe he spoke with his hands... Maybe... Oh, forget it. You're upset and I'm not helping."

"Goddamned right I'm upset!"

The Razor clasps his hands together, signaling the end of the exhibit, "We should split up. Cover more ground."

Tommy looks around, trying to focus down the poorly lit paths. Not sure which direction leads to death and which to salvation, he turns to The Razor and warns him, "Don't do something stupid."

"Of course not, Tommy," The Razor says submissively with his hands still clasped.

Tommy goes through his mental checklist aloud, "I promised Ellie I would bring back everything. The knife, the money... the balls..."

"The balls?" The Razor inquires, then remembers. "Ah, yes, of course. The Boss loves his free range, farm to table."

"Pardon?" Tommy inquires as he stares at The Razor sideways.

Staying with his scholarly tone, "Farm to table. It's more of a spiritual revelation than a cooking revolution. People of power like to control the entire life cycle of what they consume. It ensures purity."

Shrugging, Tommy seems to grasp The Razor's reasoning, "Yeah... I knew there had to be legitimate reason for his insatiable appetite for other men's privates."

"You are what you eat," The Razor recites.

# Chapter 20

# Strange Bedfellows

The gunshots and screams piercing his skull may be rattling his nerves, but it's The Razor's handiwork that has him petrified. Flinching at a mole scurrying in the bushes, Vassy finds himself spinning and ducking more than an MMA fighter losing a title bout he thought he'd win with a one-punch knockout. *I should have called for backup! You greedy fuck! Pooty's probably dead along with my career... Maybe if I just walk, I can pretend Putin left me at the market to follow another lead? Yes! That's it! If he's still alive, it's his word verse mine... No... That will never work. At best my career will be over. I'll need to make sure he's dead... Sorry, muchacho, but it's time to break up the team.*

A scream over the hill, no more than fifty feet away forces Vassy to his belly. With his gun trained at the hill's crest in the prone position, Vassy awaits The Razor. Partially hidden behind the ornamental shrubbery that adorns the path, Vassy figures The Razor, even with his heightened senses, won't be able to detect him until he's almost upon him, affording Vassy the ability to unload two, possibly three quick rounds from close range. Committing to the compromised position of lying down will mean he needs to hit his target true, for he's in no position to commence shape-shifting, evasive maneuvers if it becomes close quarters combat.

As the figure power walks into the open, the moonlit gleaming blade of the scepter partially lights up the silhouette of the psychopath.

Firing off a successful shot with his Glock 9mm in the prone position from behind the barbed branches of an ornamental bush would have been hard enough during the day; in low levels of night light, it was next to impossible. Adding to the level of difficulty, not only was it more difficult to see due to the time of day, the heat and humidity were wreaking havoc on his aim as well, for huge burning droplets of sweat were currently cascading into his one open eye, making a tricky shot, a shot in the dark...

At twenty-five feet away the outline of the madman begins to take shape. The Razor has lost his hat somewhere along the way and is about a foot short... *Wait, who the fuck is that? Dunlop? No limp... Wait a minute...* Realizing that it's definitely not The Razor in his sights, Vassy turns his aim up the hill to see if The Razor is following behind Dunlop, wisely utilizing him as a decoy. When The Razor fails to crest the ridge, fear paralyzes Vassy. *He's fucking behind me... Shit!* Spinning on the ground, Vassy sweeps his weapon in the opposite direction—nothing! Sensing imminent danger, he rolls back over and springs to his knees, doing his damnedest to re-engage the target. Dunlop is less than fifteen feet away, and walking directly towards him with the scepter held high, when he reengages him. As Vassy trains his 9mm on the bridge of his nose, Dunlop's sneer screams foul. Vassy can't help but smirk at the jerk, who is as clearly dumbfounded by Vassy's dexterity as the average arrogant punk was when they squared off with the "Vassinator".

"Freeze!" Vassy screams.

"I'm frozen," Dunlop announces annoyedly as he resets his posture and facial features.

Hopping to his feet, Vassy retrains his weapon as he stammers forward almost tripping on the bush he just used for cover, "On the ground!"

Dunlop rolls his eyes, "Should I freeze, or get on the ground?"

Stopping within six feet of Dunlop, Vassy's hands shake wildly, making for an extremely itchy trigger finger, "Fuck with me Mighty Cong and I'll blow your head clean off!"

Dunlop seems way too cool for the weather and circumstances, "Speaking of blowing your head clean off, I wish I could recommend a service I recently received."

"You kill that hooker?"

Dunlop doesn't answer, but rather offers Vassy the gleam in his eyes of a child being questioned on whether he was the one who fingered the cream cheese frosting of a freshly baked carrot cake.

Vassy does a quick look around for The Razor before he asks again, "Did you kill that hooker?"

A sheepish Dunlop answers, "Guilty."

Vassy's eyes go wild, and he extends his arms, locking his elbows and cocking the Glock, "You sick fuck! You're going to jail for the rest of your fucking life!"

Dunlop seems to be taken back by the outlandish statement, "Am I?"

"Yes!" Vassy confirms.

"Why?"

Shocked into rage, Vassy debates killing him and worrying about the collateral damage later, "'Cause, that's what they do with cold-blooded murderers. They put them in jail."

Dunlop seems to process the statement, but then adds it to other points in his mind. Finally looking around and shaking his head in disagreement, "But for that to happen, you'll have to report this... All of this. And then, you wouldn't get this…" Raising the scepter, Dunlop looks at Vassy with a knowing smile. "And let's be honest, you want this almost as much as you want The Razor."

Spitting at Dunlop's feet, Vassy is disgusted by Dunlop's logic tree, "You know jack-shit Dunlop."

Downplaying Vassy's dress-down, Dunlop is rather detached in his dissertation, "Actually Detective, I'm a Professor… Which means I'm most likely far more educated than a simpleton such as yourself, or your prehistoric partner for that matter."

Vassy can't help but chuckle, "I hope for your sake, you're more tactful with your cellmate."

Dunlop doesn't seem to mind the chide, "Let me go tonight and I'll give you two of the three things you wanted since you woke this morning. Not a bad day's catch…"

"You have no idea what I want, asshole."

Dunlop offers Vassy a shit-eatin' grin along with an assumption, "Here's a shot in the dark… The Razor, the scepter, and the money."

Vassy somewhat concedes with a simple nod of his head, but then adds, "You forgot to add yourself to the list, Professor."

"No I didn't, for you never wanted me. You were going to arrest me, but you never wanted me. Right? What you really want is The Razor, and I can understand and appreciate why."

Looking around Dunlop once again for a trailing Razor, Vassy decides to start moving to his right slowly as to better his chances in case Dunlop decides to run or strike, "You trying to get inside my head, Professor? You teach archaeology, or psychology?"

Dunlop notices his tactical maneuver, but seems to brush it off for the basic training that it is. "I lecture actually, and perform field work from time to time."

Setting his feet, Vassy feels more comfortable at the angle and distance he's created between himself and the target area, "Field work? Sounds impressive. Like Indiana Jones?"

Not turning the forty-five degrees to his left, which would put him face to face with Vassy once again, Dunlop decides to speak straight ahead as if he's lecturing his class, instead of his captor, "Actually yes."

"Let me guess. That's why you're out here tonight? Field work?"

Smiling broadly, Dunlop responds with a resounding, "Precisely."

Vassy shrugs, "I guess we're both lucky I just happened to stumble upon you…"

"Thank goodness you came, Detective. I was growing concerned that-"

"Save it! Hand over the knife!" Vassy demands.

"Are you referring to the scepter?" Dunlop counters cutely.

"Sword, knife—septic, whatever! Just hand it over!!"

Slowly turning his head to Vassy, but not his body, Dunlop forces eye contact, "I can't do that."

"Then I'll just have to kill you."

Dunlop let's out a large exhale, "I'll happily oblige your request after I receive payment."

"I'm taking that too… Sorry, Professor, but it's clear you don't lecture business classes at the University, for you'd realize I'm holding all the cards."

"Except the trump card," Dunlop asserts.

"And that is?" Vassy inquires with genuine curiosity.

"Me," Dunlop declares with a wink.

Flabbergasted, Vassy admonishes, "You? I'm the one holding the gun."

Dunlop acquiesces a nod, but follows with his own pertinent fact, "But I'm the loadstone for both The Razor and the buyer."

Vassy weighs the Professor's point, "Going one for three tonight would be just fine with me."

Dunlop turns his body, facing Vassy, forcing him to either move, or concede the advantage, "This isn't baseball, Detective. We both know it's all, or nothing. The Razor will lodge this scepter in your chest by week's end—that's if my buyers don't get to you first."

Closing his eyes briefly to block the pain of the truth, Vassy is noticeably weakened by the visual, "Talk."

"The buyer has a million. This scepter is worth ten. Killing The Razor, priceless…"

"Keep going," Vassy prompts.

"We both know, regardless of what else transpires tonight, you need to kill The Razor. The only question is, what would you rather have? Cash or credit?"

"What would you take if you were me?" Vassy probes.

"The money."

"Then I'll take the knife," Vassy insists.

Shrugging acceptance, Dunlop replies, "Fair enough."

"Giving up that easily? Just like that?" Vassy berates.

Seemingly befuddled by Vassy's scolding criticism, Dunlop asks, "What do you mean?"

"Why don't you want the knife, if it's so valuable?" Vassy asks as he points to it with his chin.

"I came here to sell the SCEPTER for a million dollars. I'm content with that."

Vassy's eyes furrow, "If it's worth so much more, why sell it for just a million?"

"Well, as you so keenly pointed out earlier, I don't teach business, but I do understand basic economics. In this case, charge what the market will bear."

Vassy digests the dissertation, "On second thought, keep your fucking knife, scepter, whatever the fuck it is. I wouldn't know who to sell it to anyways."

"Fair enough. I need something to protect me while we work your wish list."

Vassy lowers his gun, "Where are you supposed to make the drop?"

"Far side of the park. There's some kind of a formal stone garden and/or statue?"

"I know exactly where that is. Let's move."

Smiling warmly, "I love field work."

## Chapter 21

## From Unfolding to Unraveling

It's been only fifteen minutes, max, since he separated from Vassy, but Putin is feeling more than just a little nostalgic for his dastardly dispositioned partner and their estranged relationship. Barely co-existing at best, would be better than being alone right now and with giving his word that back-up wouldn't be called, Putin feels backed into a corner, even though he's got open space in every direction. Dark open space is great when you're running from something, but not so ideal for finding something. Something... That's what's got Putin in such a panic. His cop instincts are screaming at him to run at a full sprint to his ride, and flee the scene like he's driving the getaway car to a bank job gone wrong. Get his family and make an impromptu visit to his long-lost relatives in the Ukraine and learn to love farming rocky soil for the next ten years.

But as he tries in vain to silence his nerves, the distant, and sometimes not so distant, screams of grown men pierce his fragile veil. Men are murdering and being murdered all over, and he knows it's only a matter of moments before he's going to be either the former or the latter. He's also praying the police will be coming sooner than later, for the cries and gunshots that have soiled the steamy air over the last ten minutes surely must have traveled in the humidity ten miles in either direction. Then the lights go out.

*Oh shit... Please don't tell me this is a blackout?* But before he can answer his own question, car horns and screams in the far distance tell him the boys in blue will be far too busy within the inner city to check out noise violations in the park.

With nothing more than the moon and stars to guide him, he stumbles like a town drunk through a thicket of evergreen bushes to avoid the main path that most likely has someone waiting for something. Guilt suffocates his soul, constricting his ability to reason, as he comes to grips with the fact that his countless countermeasures to remain undetected have resulted in inexcusable inaction. Inaction that has surely seen several innocent civilians slaughtered, outside of the gang members, who, regardless of their chosen career paths, are protected by the oath he took so many years ago to serve. Luckily his sanity has made the argument that the means to an end are justified in this case, for if he gets killed, he can't kill, and clearly, eventually, tonight, he'll be killing. That sober truth stops him in his tracks and forces him to have a come-to-Jesus conversation with himself.

*Snap the fuck out of it, Pooty! Everyone in this park is an animal, and there's only two types of animals, predators and prey. You're a predator! You hunt! No one fucking hunts me. I'm here to establish my position on the pyramid. This is for Maggie and the kids. Daddy's coming home with blood on his hands, but I'll wash them along with the money I launder from this night. Time to shine…*

Renewed in his conviction, cleansed of his impending crimes, and bailed out by God of his moral bankruptcy, Putin checks his piece, then taps his chest pocket that holds his two spare clips. Satisfied with the heat check, Putin begins to stalk the night. Fully adjusted to the moonlit landscape, Putin's steps are sure-footed as he continually acquires potential threats in front of him, instead of feeling threatened by shadows behind him.

It's only a matter of moments before he sees a silhouette of a large person lying on the ground a couple of yards from a park bench. From his distance of forty feet, he can't tell for sure if the person is lying still because he or she is dead, or because he's doing a poor job of hiding. As Putin ponders the possibilities that must have led to the person being in the prone position, he settles on the likely scenario that he'd been in the middle of stalking someone who must be just out of Putin's visual canopy, and has had to drop quickly to take cover, failing to take his exposed backside into consideration.

Putin encompasses the entire battlefield when formulating his plan of attack, for if the person is lying in wait, it would mean that whoever he's hiding from is on the opposite side of the park bench. After solidifying a plan A, B and C, as well as any and all contingencies, Putin settles on a quick, crouched pace. Bent over more than he'd like, Putin is diligent in his terrain sweeps, as he silently stalks his first victim, making sure to identify where the head and feet are. Coming from the direction of the feet, he aims at the figure's head. If it moves, he's committed to the kill shot. Toggling between the head and the hill twenty-five paces in front of the bench on the other side of the path, Putin gets within ten feet of the body before he can perform a quality threat assessment.

The body is no longer a threat, but whatever had mangled the once well-dressed gangster is possibly the most frightening foe Putin will ever face. Burying a sprinkler flag in each eye was the very definition of 'overkill'. Where The Razor could be now was anyone's guess. The easy answer was looking for whatever he couldn't find at the market. The real question Putin ponders, does he know he's currently being hunted by Vassy and himself, along with the other Families? Putin comes to the stark realization that it's a moot point, for The Razor knows enough to kill everything that moves, regardless if that person is looking for him, or Orion.

What's got Putin stumped is if The Razor is such a highly-trained assassin, why has he wasted so much time and energy on a single kill? The six-foot something, three hundred-plus-pound Sicilian looks to have been alive when his eyes were stabbed with the thin metal rods, due to the pure anguish on his face. The Razor would have had to sit on the man's chest as he punctured each retina. Why would he rip his shirt open as if this fight was anything but one-sided? In order to accomplish this execution, he had to have had his knees in his armpits, with some major damage to the gangster's lower limbs to allow him the leverage needed to keep him stationary during the stabbing. The gangster was big, and not just fat, meaning it had to have taken considerable concentration to render him immobile, to where he could've made the precise punctures. Regardless of The Razor's fighting prowess, this extracurricular activity seemed out of place—almost like two individuals attacked him, in succession. But The Razor worked alone… and Tommy punched, not scratched. Scratched was an understatement; the once fine Italian silk shirt was shredded like he'd been attacked by a lion, escaped from the Bronx Zoo. Tommy would have had no part in this, and to be fair to The Razor, he was nasty, but precise—a surgeon, not a butcher. He'd possibly do the eyes, but not the gouges.

Stumped, Putin can't work the murder scene out. *Maybe The Razor was infuriated that this poor sap wasn't Professor Dunlop, and took his frustrations out?* In the end, Putin decides the night's heat was oppressive enough to make everything intolerable, even something you loved to do. As he moves on from the victim, he takes one last glance at the dual yellow plastic flags that protrude from each eye socket. The deep gullies created by the gangster's hands and feet as he squirmed, confirm the worst—the man was purposely kept alive when mutilated. *Is that a TAG? Sweet piece...*

## Chapter 21.25

With his pace quickening with each gunshot, scream, or off-in-the-distance siren, Vassy's no longer sure whether it's the weather, or the wear that's got him sweating bullets. Sharp stings from beadlets off his brow burn his eyeballs, forcing him to squint when the light restrictions are forcing him to walk wide eyed. His outlook dims with the city-wide blackout that flicks the switch on the park and his patience. *Fuck!*

Dunlop doesn't slow a step, relishing the new curveball thrown their way. "What a sky!"

Vassy is in no mood for the bright-eyed, bushy-tailed traveler, "Make a right after those hedges."

"I'm really forming a lather!" Dunlop exclaims before enthusiastically following his marching orders.

"A lather?" Vassy repeats rhetorically. Under his breath, Vassy mutters his displeasure for his traveling companion's carefree disposition, "Fucking white people…"

"With the lights out, no one will see us coming!" Dunlop proclaims.

"With your loud fucking mouth, they'll hear us long before they see us!" Vassy scolds.

"Sorry! I mean, sorry…" Dunlop finishes in the lowest octave humanly possible.

## Chapter 21.50

*This is how nature intended it! The thrill of the hunt, Mr. Dunlop. I'm coming for you, but who are you really? Circumstances have changed and you have clearly changed with them, to say the least. I can't help but feel admiration for your uncanny ability to crawl from the depths of Hell and rise... Aha! Hell... That's it! Isn't it? Have you seen the other side? You must have... Your taint tantalizes me... Is that why I want you so badly? Why I cannot stop thinking of you? I'm obsessed with you, you know. Why? You're more than just another job aren't you... Are we kindred spirits? Are you my long-lost brother, Mr. Dunlop? I never forgave her for giving you away...*

Squatting on a sturdy branch of a thick maple tree, twelve feet from the ground, The Razor surveys the field of play from his predator's perch. Concealed by the tree's canopy, The Razor can see out quite clearly, while the unsuspecting gangsters and gangbangers stumble about completely unaware of his presence. Waiting absolutely still, ready to pounce, The Razor mimics a spider on the edge of her web, appearing disinterested, or even possibly asleep. As a 4th Street Latino jogs directly towards him, The Razor knows he cannot see him, for if he did, he would have started shooting by now. Whether he's planning to use the tree for a bathroom break, cover, or for a superior vantage point, he'll look up once he arrives at the base. A crescent moon smile shines sinisterly on The Razor, as all three possibilities lead to the same end game, the gangbanger's end.

*Whether you've been to Hell, or are from it, I'm about to give you the chance to go back to it, for it's time to die, Mr. Dunlop.*

Upon his approach, the Latino slows to a tentative trot as he begins to scan the area, ensuring no one sees him entering his new hiding spot. The Razor can appreciate his apprehension. The last thing the gangbanger needs is for someone to witness his ascent into the impromptu tree fort, for they'd be able to pluck him off a branch like a dangling overripe apple.

*But before I deliver your soul to Satan, or your testicles to Ellie, I must deliver my message to the masses.*

The twenty-four-year-old Latino staggers to the base of the tree. Bent over at the trunk's base, he's more than just winded, he's gasping for air. Cigarette serrated lungs that can barely supply enough oxygen to the young man's body to conquer the dilapidated stairwell to his 5$^{th}$ floor, low rent studio, are clearly not up to the task of sprinting back and forth in weather that's both 99 degrees hot and 99 percent humid. Taking a moment to clear his lungs and mind, the gangbanger commits to exposing himself for the short duration that the climb's new vantage point will afford him. With his head lowered in contemplation, the man appears to be praying to the statue-still Razor standing ten feet above him.

*What would you do if you were me right now, Mr. Dunlop? What would Father do?*

The Razor slowly and silently removes his long blade from his body sheath, conscious of the moon's reflection off its shined sides. Before he raises the knife above his head, he relishes in a long, hypnotic whiff of the blade's edge, like a store manager inspecting a crate of fresh tomatoes from a local farmer. The smell of cold steel, the faint residue of iron left behind from years of dried blood… The knife's distinct odors fill The Razor with a warm, palatable comfort. Admiration for the inanimate object makes the knife less of a weapon wielded, and more of a partner in crime.

"I think a child's innate desire to climb a tree, is derived from Man's original desire to descend from the tree as an ape."

Still out of breath, the Latino stops breathing entirely. Frozen solid, like the moth on a web that's just detected the spider's first tentative touch. Snapping his head back upon configuring the Razor's position, the Latino's pupils, though adjusted wide-eyed for the moonlight, aren't able to fully dilate to the diameter needed to discern between the dark wood branches and The Razor's black suit.

"My Father never built me a treehouse."

The Latino fumbles clumsily for his gun, forcing his face from The Razor in order to concentrate on freeing the trigger hook from the frayed front loop of his jeans. The Razor drops out of the tree like a falling limb upon the much smaller, exhausted, and discombobulated gangbanger. With the knife gripped tightly in both hands and pointing downwards, the blade dives deep into the man's left shoulder, severing the Carotid artery, and splaying the heart from the top, down. The man's death is instantaneous, with only the sound of a Whoopie cushion and subsequent smell emanating from his bent over buttocks signaling his bodily function failure.

"I forgave him for his empty promises, but not for his treatment of my mother and me."

Looking down upon the bent-over form of the dead man, The Razor helps the man's head back as he smooths his blood-soaked hair behind his ears, "Gandhi once said, 'Be the change you wish to see in the world.'"

Gazing longingly for a sacred moment into the dead doll-eyes of his latest faceless victim, The Razor gently closes them both with one soft hand, hovering his cupped palm an inch over the man's lips, possibly to feel a breath, or catch a soul... Neither tries to escape, and he loses interest. Abruptly releasing the held head, The Razor collects himself as he erects himself, becoming resolute, "I'm going to lead by example, Father. Not just say, but do..."

## Chapter 21.75

Vinny Pizzovannie had a splitting headache since yesterday. High blood pressure and a low pain threshold weren't helping his mood. The stroll through the park would have been taxing enough had he'd simply been given orders to hunt one of the most dangerous men on the planet. Add the high stakes to the game, and the ruthless nature of the expected collateral damage, and Vinny was having a hard time seeing straight. On a good day, the stifling heat and humidity would have stopped him at the first park bench had it not been for the promise he made before the Creator to avenge his close friend's cold-blooded murder. Not only had Louie the Leopard been viciously slaughtered like a pig, he'd been left to bleed out like one, on the same floor that pigs and other foods were left to rot—the back storeroom. The insult to injury was on such a scandalous scale that grown men, who had spent a career killing, were shocked to silence and sniffles, for they saw themselves laying in that pool of blood, gutted. The code of conduct that a lieutenant was afforded had been thrown out the window. Even the fucking Krauts in WWII held true to the Geneva Code for the most part. But this? This was a complete breakdown in decorum.

*Louie, you fucking stunad, cocksucking, bastard ... You know you brought this on yourself, just like you always did, and now you gots me sweating my fucking balls off? This whole fucking outing is my balls! Who's calling the shots around here anyways? Some fucking Piker is, is who. Who's gonna fish from our boat if we both get killed today? You eva think of me once? You know I get chafing as soon as I start sweating. I couldn't walk with yous to the barber shop this morning, because of my chafing, and now I'm looking like a rodeo clown. A fucking clown, Louie! I feel like a fucking clown too. I've paid my dues with interest and now I'm here, answering to some chowda mouth below my rank from another Family? You fucking owe me big time, Louie. Big Time!*

Devastated over the loss of his dearest of childhood friends and longtime business partner, Louie the Leopard, Vinny Pizzovannie, aka, V.P., knows the mission's directives are unobtainable, and the cost of failure far too high. Men who are completely removed from the reality of the situation, have made poor decisions with other people's lives in haste, with the long-term ramifications of tonight's actions resulting in a wartorn Bronx for generations to come. In addition to going to war with the savage 4$^{th}$ Street Latinos, a group with whom the Mob currently profited from a symbiotic business relationship, the Mob was about to commit atrocities tonight that it hadn't dared do in over hundred years— slaughter innocent people.

Once the Mob crossed that line, it would not be able to come back. Not only would it finally lose the PR battle with the Feds in the press, it would also lose all the street cred it built up over generations with the public. The romance of all things Mafia would forever be over, and his beloved family would find itself affronted by every do-gooder, aspiring politician, and vigilante that the Internet could muster.

They'd be fighting on all fronts, and the reason? No one was really sure, other than there was some priceless piece of artwork that no one had seen, or could even authenticate as existing. As Vinny weighs the pros and cons, he's at peace with killing tonight. It's the here and now that leaves him questioning the call. The blaring fact that innocent people will most definitely die in the process claws at his conscience. *Haven't enough innocent people already died because of him?* As the questions and subsequent frustrations mount up, due to the clear lack of answers, Vinny finds himself in a conundrum; does he stay in the park and follow orders he knows are a clear violation of his ethical oath, or does he abandon his Family, which would also be a clear violation of his ethical oath?

A romantic couple strolling the lamplit path forces his hand as they wave in his direction, acknowledging his presence, as people approaching in low levels of light often do. He raises his left hand out of habit, bringing his right hand to his left jacket breast out of habit as well. His gun hides underneath his lapel, but so does an aching heart. He holds his hand to his heart, but the sheathed gun lays between his palm and chest, muffling the ribcage rattling thumps of his heaving heart.

*Oh, for Christ's sake kids, I'm so sorry… See you in Hell, Louie, see you in Hell…*

## Chapter 22

## I Could Have Been a Contender

Though quick of wit and hand-eye coordination, Vassy's uncanny burst of speed and strength isn't complemented by marathon endurance. In the end, Vassy's nothing more than an out-of-shape, fifty-something, part-time smoker, with the cardio capacity of a biker bar bouncer. After his initial burst of speed, he's nothing more than an imported leather suitcase on stumps. His lack of aerobic abilities, coupled with the extreme heat and humidity of the stymieing evening air, makes the short jaunt an epic adventure. Climbing the last hill feels like reaching the summit of a mountain, and Vassy's well-insulated kidneys produce crippling pain. The distance between himself and Dunlop grows with every stride, and Vassy knows that the pounding in his head won't retreat until he lessens the pounding the ground's taking from his heavily fatigued fat feet. He desperately needs to gain control of the situation before it literally gets away from him. Though he needs to slow his pace in order to slow his heart rate, it's his spunky new sidekick who would need to make the first move.

Between gulps of air, Vassy directs, "Hold up!"

Dunlop stops, and cranes his head backwards in annoyance, "Don't you guys have to pass a physical?"

"Fuck you! I've been under the weather for the past week."

Turning to Vassy, Dunlop stands before him with his hands on his hips, chest heaving heavily. His powerful posture and sinister sneer are just part of Dunlop's transformation from the weak, pathetic professor whom Vassy had apprehended earlier, to an imposing opponent.

Holding one hand up to Dunlop as he bends over to brace for another pulse of pain, Vassy speaks between labored breaths, "Alright Dunlop. Let's go through this again. What do you do when we meet the buyer?"

"I still say it's a massive mistake for you to be with me."

"For the last fucking time! I'm not letting you out of my sight!"

Casually removing his left hand from his hip, Dunlop extends it to Vassy with the palm out and fingers raised, "I'm not saying, let me meet him in Connecticut, I'm saying give us-"

"Enough!" Vassy shoots back, "I'm the one with the experience here! You want to tell me what part of the world that thing came from—fine! You want to tell me how much it's worth—fine! But don't tell me how to sell it illegally. That's my cup of tea."

Dunlop seems genuinely tickled by Vassy's choice of words, "That's funny."

Still bent over, Vassy seems insulted, "What's so funny?"

"Cup of tea…"

Vassy forces his frame to the erect position, clearly self-conscious of Dunlop's jab, "Why's that funny? I'm not international enough to use—"

**BANG!**

Vassy's face explodes as a bullet from a mobster's gun, which had entered from the lower back of his skull, furiously forces its way out. Vassy drops like a bag of sand. Behind him, the mobster analyzes the scene, somewhat stunned by the savagery of the shot. Taking in the lump of lard that was a law enforcement agent, the killer casually adjusts his gaze to his new target, the Professor. His eye contact with Dunlop is fleeting, for what hangs at Dunlop's side is the true twinkle of his eye. The scepter has gathered what appears to be all the park's moonlight, mesmerizing the mobster like a shiny new lure does a fish.

Dunlop looks down at the scepter, "You want this?"

The mobster keeps his eyes affixed to the scepter, like a kid staring at a train set in a holiday department store window, "Yes…"

"Here." Dunlop flings the scepter at the mobster. The scepter travels head over heel like a tomahawk, faster than physics would suggest possible. The scepter lodges itself with a deep thud in the mobster's chest, splitting his sternum like a coconut. But instead of a white watery substance pouring out, a red syrup erupts, spraying the surrounding shrubbery like a one-gallon water balloon dropping from a rooftop terrace.

"Wow! That was messy!" Dunlop takes a moment to take in his latest triumph. The force of the impact had knocked the mobster off his feet, where he'd landed on his back, dead long before he hit the ground. After briefly admiring yet another of his flawless victories, Dunlop struts to the body and straddles it, before kneeling down and grappling the scepter with both hands.

Looking the wide-eyed dead man's expression over, Dunlop takes on the role of field nurse, slash helicopter mom, "I'm going to remove this as quickly and painlessly as possible." Winking at the man, "Like yanking a Band Aid. Let's hope you're not hairy."

Dunlop attempts to dislodge the scepter, but it doesn't release easily. Pushing and pulling on the shaft as if it were an axe in freshly cut, ancient oak, Dunlop must coax it loose. Finally freeing the scepter from its prey, Dunlop raises the scepter in the air, examining it for the first time as an academic. *Beautiful... Powerful... Well made...* The fact that it had flown true meant it was designed as a weapon of war, as much as it was a symbol of war. Thinking back on his various kills over the course of the day, starting with Louie the Leopard, Dunlop notes the scepter's razor sharpness. *It's cut through bone like butter all day! How has it remained razor sharp for thousands of years? This looks like it was just forged... And did the Incas really have the technology to produce such a finely-forged piece of metal? If they did, this changes history! I'll be famous! I'll be rich and famous! I can't give this away... This is mine... Mine forever!*

BANG!

The searing pain in Dunlop's ribs takes his breath away. Flung forward by the force of a 45 Magnum round entering his right middle back, the bullet from Mr. Meat's gun was so powerful that it had passed through both his lung and ribcage, lodging itself in Dunlop's tweed jacket. Rolling forward from the sheer impact of the lead projectile, Dunlop rolls over twice, repositioning himself on his knees. Propping himself up with the scepter, he finds himself wheezing hard from his newly blood-flooded lung. Adrenaline pumps as hard as his heart, which will kill him sooner than later if he doesn't receive medical attention in a hurry. Looking up, he sees his adversary, leveling his weapon for the kill shot.

"Well, well, well... If it isn't my number one customer..."

"Fuck you! You dirty wetback!"

Much to his chagrin, Javier can't help but feel some respect for Dunlop, "Oh, Papi's got some fight? Nice. I like fight."

Frantic, Dunlop grasps for straws, "You want a fight? Let's fight! Come on! Drop your gun, and put up your dukes!"

Javier looks at Dunlop sideways, squinting, despite the low levels of light. "Dukes? I love white people."

Dunlop begins to get up. Now crouching and using the scepter as a mini-cane, Dunlop appears to be getting a second wind, despite not having use of a second lung.

Though impressed with Dunlop's moxy, Javier has come for retribution, not inspiration, "You hurt my business big time. Not only did you use my services and not pay, you killed my employee."

Staggering to his feet, Dunlop's sneer resembles a jack-o'-lantern in the moonlight, "Her customer service skills were appalling."

"What about her other skills? Did you blow your load?"

Smiling to himself, Dunlop accidentally shares a personal moment, "Twice actually…"

Mr. Meat's jaw muscles flex, as he cocks his head and gun, "Now, I blow your load."

Mr. Meat shoots Dunlop right in the pelvic region. Not the dick, though he was aiming for it, but mere centimeters above, clearly ruining much of Dunlop's party plans for tonight's all-out flawless victory party. Dunlop hasn't processed being shot in the dick by his whore's pimp and most likely won't anytime soon, so he does what any self-respecting newly Christened eunuch would do in his situation, he grabs what's left of his junk and howls, dropping the scepter. "Ahhhhhh! You son of a bitch!"

A sinister smile cracks Mr. Meat's face, "Three's a charm Mighty Cong."

Dunlop notices the scepter off to his side and stares at it for a moment, puzzled. He looks to Javier for answers to questions he cannot even formulate when The Razor appears out of the shadows and rams his knife through Javier's throat from behind. Mr. Meat drops his gun as he frantically grabs at the razor-sharp blade protruding from his throat. His bloodied hands go limp within seconds as he drops to his knees. Propped up by The Razor's knife, Javier's lifeless eyes are crossed, focused on the blade's tip, wild fear frozen on his face. Taking his size-fourteen black boot to the back of Mr. Meat's head, The Razor uses it as leverage to yank the blade free. Once the blade is dislodged, the gang leader of the 4th Street Latinos, Javier Cruz, aka Mr. Meat, free falls face first.

The Razor momentarily admires his handiwork, before making formal introductions, "Professor Dunlop?"

Strutting slowly like a cat on a balcony railing, The Razor makes his way over to Dunlop as if he's introducing himself at an after-hours benefit being held at the Met.

"I must say, I find myself thoroughly impressed with your rapid progression. You've got a real flair for this… A certain Je n'ais se quoi, that almost humbles me."

The Razor sidesteps Dunlop, and snatches the scepter from the ground. Before Dunlop can register what has happened, The Razor retreats several feet. "Well, they say a carpenter is only as good as his tools…" Looking over the scepter with an approving eye, The Razor is awed by its evil elegance. "And this, dear Sir, is truly made for a master craftsman."

Wheezing with the last of his will, Dunlop demands the impossible, "Give it to me."

Wrenching his gaze from the object of his affection, The Razor is cordial in his answer, as he takes one last measure of the man, "But of course."

Thrusting the scepter into Dunlop's throat, he holds it there for a moment, statue steady, examining Dunlop's shock and awe expression. Seeing something worth remembering, he gives a quick yank, releasing Dunlop's body, as he claims his soul.

For all its theater, the transaction ends feeling cheap, like fondling the inside of the coin repository of a soda machine for someone else's change. Dunlop falls face down, gargling blood onto The Razor's boots. The Razor looks down, his admiration replaced with admonishment, "As a professional courtesy, I'll of course, personally inform your wife and children of your most unfortunate of endings."

Professor Dunlop shudders before lying still. Scanning Dunlop, then his boots, he lifts one boot off the ground to examine just how much blood has soaked them. Outwardly annoyed with the messiness of the matter, both physically and metaphorically, The Razor's edge is dulled by remorse, "Losing talent is a loss to any art… and you, Professor, had more promise and panache, than pomp and circumstance."

The Razor looks up, and resets his posture with a chest full of steamy summer air. Adjusting his hat with a soft touch, he finetunes the fit with a flick of the brim. Satisfied, he saunters around the pile of shit and begins to stroll along the path, only to stop suddenly, snapping his fingers. He spins with a showman's grace to face Dunlop's corpse and shoots a sly smile. Panning the prone-positioned professor until he settles on his bloodied crotch, "I hope the Boss is hungry, because you, dear chap, have quite the pair."

# Chapter 23

# Long Time, No See

Cresting the ridge, Putin is bushed. Sprinting, jogging, dropping, rolling, shooting, being shot at, and seeing dead bodies mutilated beyond recognition, has left Putin mentally, physically and emotionally spent. The fog of war has long since clouded his judgement, which he is painfully aware hasn't been the most stellar of his career as of late. Putting his career and life in jeopardy to obtain the end goal would have been more palatable, if it hadn't also, by association, put his family's lives in grave danger, as well. Knowing that the only thing between his loved ones being murdered, is him murdering, has given him a singular focus and renewed drive to get his goals accomplished, regardless of how high the hurdles might be that will surely hinder this most herculean of challenges.

Tommy, on the other hand, has gone from happenstance to his last stance. He'd spent almost the entire day having his life threatened, whether via a colleague's off-handed innuendo, or a gangster's dominant hand wielding a stiletto. Tommy is more than flustered; he is fried. Twitching, sweating, scared and tired, Tommy looks haggard and paranoid, resembling a man stumbling up his front steps with the dawn, reeking of cheap perfume, expensive scotch, and stale cigars—tearing at his lipstick-stained jacket pocket, in hopes of finding the last Benjamin of his much needed, promised paycheck.

But just like the chump trying to sneak in the kitchen window and falling on a sink full of his mother-in-law's china, Tommy knows he'd have no answers for his wife, if he was ever lucky enough to see her again. Regret weighs heavily on his soul.

The added weight, deadens his overworked legs. Looking to take a knee to catch a breath, he turns to take cover behind a bush while he regains his senses, and hopefully some common sense.

As he turns, so does Putin. The two stare for a brief moment, locking eyes long enough to read them. Neither have their guns raised at the turn, for they're both in a moment of reflection and planning. Trigger fingers itch as arms straighten like flag poles. Neither would miss from fifteen feet. Two headshots would be the extent of this gunfight. Both know the other well enough to know that the bullets had a better shot at hitting each other in mid-flight, than they did of missing their intended targets.

"Don't even think about it!" Putin warns Tommy with authority.

"I got nuttin' to lose... But you do!" Tommy fires back.

"Don't get tough with me!" Putin admonishes.

"Fuck off Pig!"

Cocking his head, Putin takes a moment to allow the insult to fully digest, before he offers a retort, "That's rather insensitive of you."

Mocking Putin's civil discord, Tommy questions, "Should I call you the "P" word?"

Putin cocks his gun, "Go to Hell."

"You both will," an English accented voice, twenty feet to Tommy's right, forewarns. Tommy instinctually acquires the new target, instantly training his weapon on the short, well-dressed fellow's chest. Partially hidden by some evergreens and an overgrown patch of daylilies, the man's stance is casual for the occasion, looking more like someone waiting for a bus than a truce. After silently cursing himself for taking his aim away from Putin, he breathes a sigh of relief when he sees Putin's laser sight locked on the newbie's heart.

With feigned chagrin, the English gentleman seems to be pleasantly surprised by his Bronx welcome. "Ahh… You two can work together after all. I had my doubts…"

Tommy and Putin wrestle with exposing themselves to each other and briefly swing their firearms back to a Mexican Stand Off. Once the show of force is displayed, both men quickly reestablish their sights on the mysterious man.

Pressed for time and patience, the gentleman reprimands them both like children, "We're wasting valuable time, Gentlemen. You're both on the same side. Mine."

"Fuck that!" Both Putin and Tommy spit simultaneously.

Pulling back on his finely-tailored hunting coat, the man smoothly extends his fingertips into short pockets of his matching tanned moleskin vest. "Oh, you have no idea. You may be the nasty cop, and you may be the loveable gangster, but you're both saints compared to what's walking around tonight."

Once again, Tommy and Putin answer as if they choreographed the confession, "The Razor."

Offering an exaggerated nod, topped off with a pursed lip, the man seems to take measure of the moment, "Ah… yes, The Razor… He would be the rather unlikeable chap who is now possessed by the Devil."

Tommy rolls his eyes and gives a half smirk to Putin, "He's a deplorable individual who loves his job, but this is the Bronx, not the Shire, and bad people do bad things."

Putin acquiesces, "The goon's right. He's nothing we can't handle."

The English gentleman turns to study Putin, who currently has his gun lazily locked on Tommy, "I'm glad 'we' is now a part of your vernacular, Detective."

Tommy becomes terse, readjusting his attention and aim on Putin, "What's he talking about?"

The gentleman is more than happy to take a break from biblical bloodshed to educate the urban caveman he made first contact with, "Vernacular is pertaining to one's-"

Cutting him off quickly, Tommy is clearly insulted, "I know what the fuck it means!"

"Oh..," the gentleman responds, slightly undignified.

Tommy takes a breath, pointing his gun from Putin to the gentleman, nudging the barrel with his pronunciation. "What does he mean by 'Detective'?"

Oddly embarrassed, Putin can't help but crack a thin smile, "I got promoted."

With genuine excitement in his voice Tommy asks, "When?"

"Last month."

"Congrats!" Tommy jubilates.

Putin's face has gained some additional color, which seems more linked to an emotional state, than a physical one. "Thanks. It's been crazy ever since. I haven't even slept since the promotion, let alone had time to reflect."

"You know, it would have been nice to celebrate with you. I feel like the fool once again, not knowing these things," Tommy whines.

Putin can't help but experience empathy, and responds in kind, "Nothing personal…"

His cordial remark hits a nerve with Tommy, and he flies off the handle, "Nothing personal. That's the second time you've disrespected me! The third if you count what you just said!"

Putin closes his eyes, and raises both hands in the air, "Don't even!"

Tommy isn't about to let him get off that easy, "Fuck dat! You know how embarrassing it was to be the only Family in all of the fucking Bronx, not invited to your son's Christening?"

"Come on, Tommy! You know I had no choice! My fucking Captain was there, for Christ's sake!"

Blown away by the bromance-turned-jaded-lovers, the English gentleman has filled his curiosity bags with all the bullshit they'll hold, and is anxious to get his new partners up to speed, "Pardon the interruption. But it's become painfully apparent that you two are intimately familiar."

Tommy squints at the gentleman for a moment, before taking four large strides towards him with his gun trained on the Englishman's right hand, which is no longer being supported by the front finger pocket of his off-season hunting vest, but rather held behind his back, cocked at the elbow, alerting Tommy that the Englishman is now most likely concealing a weapon. "You calling me a faggot?" Tommy prods.

Rolling his eyes, Putin clears his throat, "He's my second cousin."

Not looking back, Tommy quickly corrects him, "Once removed."

"And you're gonna be permanently removed, if you don't drop your fucking piece," Putin cautions.

With his gun still trained on the Englishman, Tommy turns towards Putin, cocking his head with his gun, "You threatening me? You little shit! I've saved your ass more times than I can count."

"That's not saying much…"

"Fuck you Poots! What would you look like if I let Joey and his brothers act upon their disapproval of your feelings towards Franny?"

"We were eight, Tommy!"

"How old were we when the Family was up in arms about Maggie marrying, not only outside of the Family, but outside of Italy… to a fucking Ukrainian, no less." Turning back to the Englishman, "You know this asshole isn't even a real Russian?"

"Enough! For the love of light! We're about to go to war with Satan himself. Do you understand!"

Tommy can't help but be a little insulted by the newcomer's clear lack of faith in him, and it triggers the insecurity issues he's had all day in regard to The Razor, "We can handle The Razor for the last time, whomever the fuck you are."

Putin seems to remember something that's been nagging him for longer than he can remember, "Come to think of it… Who are you and where're you from?"

The well-dressed, fit, fifty-something-year-old scholar, who looks to have jumped right off the pages of an Orvis catalogue, makes a formal introduction that he's clearly taken great pride boasting on more than one occasion, "My name is Sir Roberts Winthrop, the Third."

Tommy smiles, "Sir? You a knight?"

Sir Roberts can clearly see Tommy is amused by the title, "I was knighted..."

"Get the fuck outta here!" Tommy hoots.

Snapping his fingers, Putin points at Sir Roberts, "You… You're the buyer! Tea for two. Your email."

Rolling his eyes, Sir Roberts hopes his sarcasm isn't lost on his two new comrades, "Brilliant…"

"You're under arrest. You have the right—"

Shocked, Sir Roberts is exacerbated, "I thought he was the dumb one!"

"Watch it, Sir Knighting Gale," an annoyed Tommy admonishes.

Looking to each of them in complete frustration, "How can I possibly convey the gravity of the situation to a pair of gun-toting hooligans, who are arguing over past social faux pas?"

"I'd suggest more succinctly than whatever you just said," Putin chides.

Sir Roberts takes a deep breath and closes his eyes, before he opens his mouth, "The man you knew as The Razor, as bad as he may have been, is now the literal embodiment of Satan. Satan—yes—Satan, Gentlemen, the very king of the Underworld, will channel his power, cunning, and hatred through your Mr. Razor to take over the world!"

"Come again?" Putin and Tommy respond in unison.

"The Razor is now the Hitman from Hell."

# Chapter 24

# Deal with the Devil

Screams just over the hill send chills through both men, despite the stifling humidity. Kenny Kitchens and his beloved childhood friend, Benny Big Band, were two gangsters not only past their primes, but past their bedtimes. Haggard and spooked, both men are at their wits' end, flinching from the mere buzzing of a mosquito, scouring the park for a sweaty snack. They'd seen and done things throughout their lives that had been witnessed by normal people only in the movies. And though both men prayed nightly to the Lord in hopes that he truly forgave all souls who begged, both knew what was unfolding in Pelham Park stretched the boundaries of even the Lord's benevolence.

"I can't fucking believe this, Kenny..."

"We're not young anymore, that's for sure," Kenny replies as he unbuttons the top of his sweat-soaked dress shirt.

"I can't believe all the gunshots and screams... for Christ's sake Kenny. I thought this would be a walk in the park."

Whisking a huge wave of sweat from his forehead with his unbuttoned sleeve, Kenny's nervous twitch resembles an unmedicated Tourette's episode, "Something's been wrong since the get-go, Benny. The Razor... I feel like he's watching our every move."

Benny seems to take strength in Kenny's weakness. Being there for the other man allows Benny to momentarily remove himself from the situation, as he offers emotional encouragement, "Don't let the night get to you. You'll be looking over your shoulder until you're walking backwards."

As Benny lends love to Kenny, The Razor silently stalks them. Trailing mere steps behind the men, The Razor matches their pace, footfall for footfall, keeping his shadow inside theirs. The humidity helps mask The Razor's breath on Benny's back. Panicked and panting, pools of sweat form in each eye well and eardrum, making detecting anything other than something touching the skin, problematic. Focused on dark objects in the foreground that seem to shape shift in the shadows, neither man finds it easy to traverse a moonlit path.

"It's like he's orchestrated this whole thing for his sick fucking pleasure," Kenny carps.

The Razor thrusts his blade through the back of Kenny's neck. The powerful attack's inertia carries Kenny forward and he tumbles towards the ground. Before Benny can swing his gun around, The Razor grabs his arm at the wrist and elbow, and snaps it like a twig. Benny riles in pain as he drops his gun. The Razor quickly claims his other arm, slamming it up into his shoulder, snapping his collarbone. Before Benny can begin his cry for help, The Razor spins him from his limp arm, and delivers a decisive blow to his exposed belly, knocking the wind from him. Benny drops to his knees, stunned and silent, helpless as his dear friend claws at the massive knife lodged in the back of his head.

As Kenny's life leaves, Benny regains his breath, "Kenny!! No!!!"

"Kenny? Kenny Kitchens? Wow, he looks like he could use a remodel..."

Benny, trembling with fear, rage, and pain, stutters, "You son of a bitch! You'll pay!"

Still standing behind Benny, The Razor adjusts his hat, "Dearly, I'm sure…"

Benny has no control of his arms. His left forearm has been snapped clean, and his right arm is numb at the shoulder. Tingling in his hand tells him he'll eventually get movement back, but for now he's not winning a fistfight with Stephen Hawking. He responds to his predicament by relying on his years of training—when in doubt, tout, "Every fucking Family from here to Sicily will be looking for you. You're dead!"

Casually walking around the bent-knee Benny, The Razor is smug, "Actually, I'm more alive than ever before, but I'm no longer who you think I am."

After The Razor circles around, he makes sure to step right up to Benny, daring him to try something sneaky. His crotch now level with Benny's face, forces Benny to crane his neck up when addressing The Razor, "I think you're a fucking psycho!"

Nodding, while pursing his lips, "I think you have a poor image of me."

Regaining his composure, Benny spits on The Razor's shoes as he gives him some direction, "Go to Hell, Razor."

"Actually, I just got back."

Benny's seen enough of these situations to know it's going to end ugly, "If you're gonna do this, have some fucking professional courtesy, and be done with it!"

The Razor looks down for the first time, somewhat amused by his opponent's request, "Where's the fun in that?"

Benny tries to spit on The Razor again, but his mouth has long since gone dry, and he must settle for the sound, "Fuck you!

You make a mockery of our profession. Dressing like an evil Dr. Seuss, destroying long-standing Family truces!"

The Razor takes a long leg backwards and reexamines his captivated audience. Massaging his chin, The Razor taps it twice before he addresses the claims. "Be who you are and say what you feel, because those who mind don't matter, and those who matter don't mind."

"What?"

Seemingly shocked by Benny's woeful inadequacies when it comes to the written word, The Razor's voice goes flat, "Doctor Seuss... You appear to have the ear of one who appreciates a rhythmic quote."

Sensing a sliver of light may extend his fight, Benny tries to stall for backup, "Hey, I'll make you a deal..."

"I'm all ears, but I got to warn you, necessity never made a good bargain."

Taken back by The Razor's seeming willingness to negotiate, Benny trips up, and he offers the farm, "You let me go, and I'll give you everything I got."

Nodding a sullen 'no', The Razor seems saddened by Benny's poor attempt to present a case, "Don't you see, you already are..." With that, The Razor unbuttons his jacket's two buttons, allowing the lapel to fall away. As the sides separate, The Razor helps it along by a simple brush of his left hand. His matching vest and the gleaming handle of the scepter are exposed. The Razor looks down at the scepter, and then to Benny, whose eyes are now transfixed on the jeweled golden handle.

Benny begins to sob, "Please... for the... love of... God..."

The Razor slowly pulls the scepter out of his pants and turns it up, resting the tip gently on his nose. After taking a deep inhale, he raises the scepter in the moonlight, admiring it like a favorite sculpture in the MOMA. Still looking up at the scepter, The Razor does his clinical best, to soothe Benny's soul. "Don't cry because it's over. Smile because it happened." The Razor rams the scepter into Benny's lower throat to the handle. Benny's mouth opens wide for one last gasp of air, but The Razor moves in quickly, sucking every last molecule of air from his lungs and throat, like a college freshman draining the remaining hit in an ice bong.

# Chapter 25

# I'm my Brother's Keeper

Walking at a snail's pace in a triangular formation, the three men have their backs to each other at five paces, slightly alternating their stances every time a scream is heard in the near distance. If the pace is making them restless, the unknown destination is making them nervous. Add the wet heat and low levels of light and ammo, and the group is on edge—a razor's edge…

"Where the fuck are we going anyway?" Tommy grumbles.

"Tommy's right. The Razor could be anywhere by now," Putin adds.

"He's here. He's going to want to kill us—especially me," Sir Roberts counters.

Stopping in his tracks, Putin looks to Sir Roberts, "Why you?"

"Because I'm one of the few people who knows what the scepter can do."

Tommy has stopped as well, and chimes in, "Yeah, well he promised to kill me before this was all said and done, and that was prior to him becoming Satan."

Putin gives an exaggerated shake to his head, "I'm having a hard time believing the whole Underworld part of this."

"It's very true, nonetheless," Sir Roberts corrects.

Tommy's had enough, "Then we should split up. He ain't going to come at us all at the same time. He's probably waiting in the bushes."

Putin surveys the immediate area, and doesn't seem to see what he's looking for, "Tommy's right. We can cover more ground that way as well."

"I can't argue with your logic, but I should take this opportunity to warn you both about a potential hazard."

"We're all ears," Tommy replies.

"Since becoming Satan, The Razor can possibly… and forgive me on my vagueness, but the texts were partially destroyed…"

"Go on!" Tommy clamors.

Sir Roberts looks back and forth between the men, before settling on his feet, "There's a strong possibility that we could be facing an army of Hell Spawn."

Putin throws up his arms, "That's it. I've had enough of this voodoo nonsense! I lost my partner tonight. His partner is on a murder rampage. And you're talking about Hell on Earth?"

Sir Roberts' arms are extended, pleading for understanding, "I know it sounds utterly absurd, but I assure you—"

Putin rests his hands on his head, looking to pull his hair out, "It sounds like you're fucking with us. That's what it sounds like. Tommy? Are you listening to this?"

Tommy seems lost and defeated. Blowing a huge exhale, he sinks to a squat, "I don't know what to think anymore…"

Putin looks to his old buddy, hoping for some much-needed clarity, "You don't know what to think? You think there's a bunch of zombies walking around the park tonight?"

"Not zombies, Detective—Hell Spawn," Sir Roberts quickly corrects.

Putin is dumbfounded, "What's the difference?"

The twenty-five-million-dollar question is answered by a lightning-quick, leaping Latino from behind the light pole. Tommy, who is already squatting from mental and physical exhaustion, falls backwards, firing off a single shot that hits the light pole's bulb. The undead 4th Street gang member rushes past Tommy on all fours, and jumps into the chest of a stunned Putin. Knocking Putin to the ground, Putin's gun flies into the ivy, next to the path. The strength of the undead warrior is astonishing; though a thin-framed human when living, the 5'7", one-hundred and fifty pound teenager is more than a handful. Putin manages to finally throw the warrior off of him, after having his shirt shredded and chest severely scratched. As the Latino goes airborne, Putin rolls several feet away in the opposite direction out of instinct. The warrior lands awkwardly, but is able to contort his body, like a Cirque de Soleil trapeze artist, bouncing back to all fours within the shadows of a drooping Japanese Maple. His left eye is missing, most likely the entry point to the fatal blow that had taken his life and soul.

Sir Roberts shoots the undead in the head. The silver hollow-tipped bullet does its job, and explodes out the back as advertised. The undead, becomes the dead before his brains finish coating the shrubbery.

As Putin scrambles to his feet, he's clearly frantic, "Holy fucking shit! Holy shit!"

Tommy doesn't even get off the ground, but scampers over to the patch of ivy where Putin's gun hopefully lays, and begins to tear into the patch, like the undead warrior tore at Putin's chest, "Motha- fucka!!!"

A gasping Sir Roberts tries in vain to take control of his breath, "The difference between Hell Spawn… and the walking dead… is, the walking dead… walk."

Putin, now on his feet, checks his chest for the extent of his injuries, "We got to call this in—contain it."

Sir Roberts will have none of it, "Are you mad? Bringing unsuspecting officers to this park will be fish in a barrel for Satan."

"We can warn them—"

Tommy walks to Putin with Putin's gun in his hand, handing it to him by the barrel. As Putin takes the weapon, Tommy rests his hand on Putin's shoulder, "Who's listening to you Pooty?"

"He's right," Sir Robert agrees. "Besides, a precinct of police could very well be the nucleus for an elite, deadly force of Hell Spawn once converted."

Putin looks at his gun and then waves it at Sir Roberts, "What the fuck are we gonna do? I'm outta ammo!"

Tommy looks at his gun in disgust, "I'm tapped too."

Sir Roberts unlatches a water skin from his utility belt and tosses it to them. Putin snatches it out of the air.

"We're out of firepower, not electrolytes," Putin chastises.

"It's Holy water… Drink deep, then splash it on your knife, or your fists, or whatever in God's name you plan to fight with, because this may make the difference. And make no mistake, Gentlemen, I do mean in God's name…"

Putin takes a big gulp and then douses his pocket knife. He tosses the skin to Tommy after Sir Roberts offers an approving nod. Shaking his head, Putin is flabbergasted, "I can't believe

I'm about to go to war with Satan wielding a Swiss Army knife."

Sir Roberts takes the water skin from Tommy after Tommy guzzles half the bag and drenches his brass knuckles and forehead.

As Sir Roberts performs a last second looksee, he doesn't offer Putin much emotional support, "I don't even have that—just my hands and feet." After taking a healthy sip, he pours water in his cupped hand and then rubs his hands together while he holds the water skin with his armpit. Then he takes the bag and hastily pours some on his feet.

Tommy takes measure of his unexpected English backup, "Well, you being a knight and all, I'd imagine you're trained for shit like this."

"There hasn't been shit like this in two thousand years," Sir Robert retorts.

A morose Putin addresses his lifelong friend, "Tommy..."

"Yo."

"I'm sorry..."

"For?"

"For shutting you out. You deserve better. You've never been nothing but good to me and Maggie."

"Say no more."

"After we rain God down on this fuckhole, I'd be honored to have you over the house for a beer."

Tommy and Putin lock massive pipes in a machismo strapped Silver Screen sequence. Hugging away all the hurt, the embrace somehow humanizes their horrific happenstance. As the men break from their hug, both well with tears. Red rimmed, Tommy's eyes are harder than a whore's heart, "It's time I reached out and touched The Razor… Again."

## Chapter 26

## Three Paths, One Destination

The Holy water was more refreshing than your average thirst quencher. Tommy had become over the years a true believer in God and desperately desired to walk in the light. He'd now made up with Pooty, which had been an albatross that had been unexpectedly set free, the weight of which turned out to be heavier on his soul than anything he'd clean-jerked at the gym. A man he'd loved since a boy, who he loved as a brother, was now his brother-in-arms. Life had come full circle and Tommy decided not to just live in the moment, but to own it, using the splash of Holy water as a second Christening.

Renewed in body, mind, and spirit, Tommy is amped. Like clubbing in his twenties, Tommy is about to out everything, everyone, and he'd be swinging until either he was the last man standing, or his arms fell off. Going down swinging on the grandest of stages was how his father would have wanted it. Carpe Diem on the Red Carpet baby! Guns were for the weak. Anyone could pull a trigger, but how many could throw a punch, or even more importantly, take one to the chops? Tommy struts along the path, shadow-boxing to loosen up the logs that swing from his bowling ball shoulders.

Hoping for action, he gets his wish, not a hundred yards from the launch point, in the form of a crazed 4th Street Latino, with a 'Curb your Dog' sign protruding from his chest. The 5'10", one-hundred and seventy-five-pound, lifetime criminal dons more tats than a pirate and more hair than Cousin It. His face on a good day would have been hard to discern through the thick black shoulder-length cut, but adding the undead element to his grooming practices, has made for a sightline less impressive than a French Poodle's. Though on a normal day, the gangbanger's ability to run in near pitch black conditions while hindered by the field of view of a WWII Bradley tank would have given Tommy pause, the fact that a two and half foot metal signpost is currently jutting straight out of his chest, like a knight's jousting pole, has frozen Tommy's reaction time.

The Hell Spawn closes the distance, approaching the speed of a Belmont thoroughbred. Tommy barely gets his fists open in time to grab the post, before it finds its home in his chest. Luckily, Tommy's unparalleled lower body strength, which connects to his upper torso, via a core muscle pack that would emasculate a yoga guru from a Himalayan village, affords Tommy the ability to literally carry the gangbanger's inertia forward and to the side. The Hell Spawn's forward momentum, in effect, aids Tommy's toss, which mimics the flight pattern of a bad guy being flung into a stack of empty cardboard boxes by B.A. Baracus.

The Hell Spawn rolls several times, which is a feat unto itself, considering the pole acts as a kickstand of sorts. Once the Hell Spawn comes to rest, it's on its feet within seconds after floundering like a freshly caught fish. Enraged by the nuisance which the pole presents, the Hell Spawn frantically yanks on it with zero regard for the self-inflicting wound it's exasperating. Clearly the rage aspect of whatever the transformation has resulted in, has taken much of the cognitive capabilities from the human. Tommy takes note in the fleeting seconds between charges that he'll have the intellectual advantage on his enemy, but most likely not the athletic advantage. Oddly enough, Tommy finds this new playing field exhilarating. Having the chance to outthink his opponent for once, instead of just outlasting him, adds an element of intrigue that causes an unexpected field of goosebumps to form along his forearms. *Oh yeah baby!*

Though a great game plan puts you in a position to win, executing the game plan wins the day, and Tommy knows that he needs to execute a kill-strike quickly, before the Hell Spawn redirects his anger back to its intended target—him. Kissing the big brass knuckles with soft, thoughtful lips, Tommy drops into a three-point stance and explodes into a bull rush. Accelerating to maximum warp within steps of his stance, Tommy treats the gangbanger like he's a QB about to throw a bomb, with Tommy coming off his blindside. Failing to compensate for his newfound physical attributes has him careening uncontrollably towards his target. In addition to overshooting his intended target, his speed to weight ratio are a poor combination for the wet grass and Italian leather loafers. Falling backwards as he begins to slide past the Hell Spawn, Tommy frantically grasps for the pole before he drops on his ass. Successful, Tommy manages to considerably lessen his fall by using the gangbanger as an airbrake. Driven to the ground with an emphatic thud, the Hell Spawn lies next to him, squirming. If he was still one of the living, he'd most likely be trying to catch his breath, or more likely bleed out, but Tommy isn't banking on normal bodily behaviors. Quickly rolling on top of the gangbanger, Tommy applies every ounce of his upper body weight to the pole, shoving the pole further inside the man, until the pole enters the soft, wet ground beneath him. The signpost's sharp metal, 10"x14" partially-rusted board, which does in fact read, *Curb Your Dog! Please*, slices through Tommy's palms, as he presses down with all his might. The gangbanger goes berserk upon the post's full pierce, desperately trying to claw, bite, and kick any part of Tommy he can make contact with. Firmly securing the signpost with his right, Tommy treats the pole like a pommel on a rodeo bronco's saddle, holding on for dear life, as his left hand ramps up the rhythm of his punch cadence, landing thirty powerful pile drivers before the gangbangers head literally implodes, sending chunks of brain in several directions. Unaware at what punch count sent the Spawn back to Hell, Tommy knows the only thing going to take over this body now are the maggots in a couple of days.

## Chapter 26.33

Putin is relieved to have finally buried the hatchet with Tommy. A hefty weight off his shoulders had injected an air in his step he hadn't felt in years. Beers with Tommy! Life was good… That's if it didn't end in the next couple of minutes due to his heart being ripped out of his body by a savage Satan soldier. Looking down at the small, foldable, utility knife he was carrying, Putin's stomach does a back flip. *What in God's name is this gonna do in a fight, regardless of the supernatural powers now bestowed upon it? Holy water… Holy fucking shit! I need to find a piece and find it quickly. But how…?*

Four shots fired in quick succession, followed by a guttural scream that's clearly cut short a couple hundred yards across the meadow to his right, answers his question. The four shots tell him the man was shooting at something, and the scream tells him he'd sadly missed his mark. Knowing that the Hell Spawn had no use for the gun, tells him he's got a piece waiting for him, if he can figure out how to evade whatever is stalking the area. Putin's a gambler by nature, but knows the odds aren't stacked in his favor regardless if it's just one beast, or worse, a pack of them. If he goes to battle with a lone Hell Spawn, he likes his odds. If he's confronted by more than one, he knows it's game over, regardless if he reaches the piece prior.

The thought of him being ripped apart and then turned into a minion of Satan, to help a horde from Hell overthrow humanity, has him trembling and tearing. A vision of him attacking his own family in their kitchen as the horde lays waste to the rest of the Bronx hits home hard. *Fuck that shit! Fight to the fucking death, Pooty! You can do this! For the kids! For Maggie...*

An anger so powerful it's palpable, pulsates from deep within Putin. Rage... Looking down at his forearms, Putin is astonished by the newly defined muscles, which have thick, throbbing arteries and veins throughout. *Was that water not just blessed, but juiced?* Setting his shoulders, Putin looks off into the night, focusing on the area of the scream, relieves himself of a huge exhale, and takes off at a full sprint.

## Chapter 26.66

Sir Roberts cannot believe the extraordinary circumstances that have him halfway around the world, walking a park in the middle of the Bronx, stalking Satan. Hell had unleashed itself on Earth, and the only backup he has to contain it is a kooky cop and an overly emotional Mob muscle man—neither of whom have a bullet between them. *How is this possible? Two trained killers, in the battle of their lives, show up to the fight for humanity with less lead than a Number 2 pencil?* Dumbfounded by their complete lack of foresight, Sir Roberts begrudgingly respects their willingness to go out in a blaze of glory, armed with nothing more than their arms.

Looking down at his own hands, he can't help but to release a hearty chuckle. He too had somehow spent his entire stockpile of ammunition. *Too many killers are out tonight...* He's keenly aware that he needs to find his mark and quickly, for sooner or later, he would be either going to Heaven or Hell. Nothing else mattered, except to get the scepter to the nearest high church and dismantle it on the altar. Could he withstand the scepter's succulent siren song?

Sir Roberts has his self-doubts, but knows there isn't another option. Already Satan is gaining power and needs only to perform a proper sacrifice to open a portal to the Underworld in which he can force the rapture. Sir Roberts' gamble on this important piece of the puzzle, had led to his decision of Pelham Park as the drop-off with Dunlop, due to the obvious choice for the ceremony that Satan would choose. If his books were correct, and he had no reason to believe they weren't, Satan would be drawn to the monolith in the middle of the park, regardless of what flesh vessel he used for the festivities.

If he could surprise Satan in the middle of the transformation, he could kill him quite easily. Comparatively speaking of course, for killing the Fallen Angel himself would never be an easy task. Having lived for more than two thousand years, having dealt with the depraved, destitute, diabolical and dysfunctional, you're more likely than not, someone who can sense a deal going south and have made the correct contingency plans. Sir Roberts knows he's got to get to the monolith, but knows he's got to allow his two unsuspecting teammates to arrive prior to him, to perform the task of decoy, drawing what surely will be a sizable security detail of demonic fiends into the open. Leading lambs to the slaughter wrenches Sir Roberts' stomach, but he's made his own deal with the Devil, and someone's got to be the sacrificial lamb. *I'll take excellent care of both your families! Your children will never want for anything! The best schools, clothing, housing... you name it. They'll know your sacrifices, your place in history. Your place next to our Holy Father... as God is my witness!*

Twenty paces up the path, a shirtless man limps into the open, moving far faster than his clearly broken left leg should allow.

Sir Roberts knows this man is no longer of the living and any pain he feels in his leg is dwarfed by the pain of his soul's eternal imprisonment. Hunched over, the man makes no eye contact, which suits Sir Roberts just fine, considering it's written that the eyes of the Hell Spawn can scare a man frozen, making him an easy kill. The man picks up speed, clearly on the attack. Sir Roberts sets his stance—half guard. He'll lean mostly on Karate for his hand-to-hand combat with the undead, since the style lends itself to creating the most distance between the foe. The last thing he wants is to be in a ground and pound position with someone trying to chew his face off. In addition to the no-holds-barred style of combat that his enemy would be utilizing, any form of combat that lends itself to a wrestling format, could leave him tied up, while another beast could show up to feast. That would be most unfortunate... No, quick chops and kicks would do the trick.

From Sir Roberts' immediate left, there is a rustling in the bushes...

# Chapter 27

# A Touching Moment

As Tommy crests yet another hill, he finds himself standing before the stone statue, The Bronx Victory Memorial, which is the centerpiece of Pelham Park. Absently flexing his left hand in the studded brass knuckles with the lead inserts, he wonders what the architect was thinking. Resembling a monolith from Rome, or the 3rd Reich, Tommy can't help but feel the weight of the stone upon his soul. As he scans from the top down once again, a familiar figure appears from behind the stone's base, The Razor. Walking with the presidential prowess of Abraham Lincoln himself, taking a stroll through the White House gardens, The Razor casually waves an overly gracious greeting. "Tommy. Beautiful night."

"Yeah… Summer breeze feels good."

"You look like you've been busy since we separated."

"Yeah…"

"Anything to report?"

"When did I start reporting to you, Asshole?"

The Razor seems to relax somewhat. Tommy's farce appears to have worked.

"Always so combative Tommy… You know why I like you?"

"I didn't think you liked me."

"On the contrary. I rather enjoy your company."

"Enough, not to kill me?"

"That depends…"

"On?"

"Loyalty… Loyalty Tommy. That's what I like about you. It's your best attribute."

"I believe I've exhibited several fine traits today, with loyalty being one of them."

"True, but the only reason I didn't kill you earlier today was because you're a loyal soldier… That alone, has kept you breathing far longer than you can appreciate."

Motioning to the scepter at The Razor's side, Tommy can't help but to show his dismay for The Razor's trophy, "I see you found Dunlop."

"Yes… Mr. Dunlop. He wasn't too happy that I took his treasure… or his testicles for that matter."

Pulling out a plastic bag from the inside of this jacket pocket, The Razor holds the bag up to the moonlight, which is filled with blood and something else…

"I'm sure you did your best to console him," Tommy sarcastically summarizes.

"He's doing much better now…" The Razor ominously answers.

"Did you also find the buyer?" Tommy inquires.

"No. I was actually hoping you had some good news for me on that front."

"Sorry, but I've been busy."

The Razor walks a little closer. "With?"

"It turns out the entire park is possessed, and subsequently, can't help but try to kill me."

The Razor walks a little closer. "Which obviously impaired your ability to find our buyer."

"Obviously."

The Razor walks a little closer. "You know Tommy… It is impossible to govern the Universe without the aid of a Supreme Being."

"I guess that's crazy talk for, you should be in charge?"

The Razor walks closer yet. Now only a couple feet from Tommy. "Actually, that's George Washington. You a fan?"

"I'm a fan of action, not words, 'cause you see… not only do actions speak louder than words, they're easier to understand."

As The Razor walks to within inches of Tommy, he inquires, "And who said that?"

"Me."

Tommy connects with a quick jab to The Razor's right cheek, knocking him back several feet. The brass knuckles sting The Razor's face due to their Holy water bath, but it's the power of the sanctified southpaw punch that has him bleeding profusely.

The Razor rubs his jaw as he looks to Tommy, now several feet away hunched, cocked, and ready to rock. "Power always thinks... that it is doing God's service when it is violating all his laws." The Razor gets into an odd erect fighting stance and smiles broadly.

"Who you quoting now, Razor?"

"John Adams. And Tommy – Please, call me Lucifer."

The Razor springs in the air towards Tommy. A former high school ice hockey goalie phenome, Tommy is quick to sidestep the sailing Satan. They swing back and forth, punch for punch; The Razor slashes Tommy in the arm with the scepter. Tommy gets a shot to The Razor's chops that dislodges a chunk of flesh from his upper lip. Back and forth they dance, with neither side losing a step.

Something scratches at Tommy's subconscious as the fight unfolds. *The Razor is pulling punches... Why? It's as if he's afraid he'll miss with that weapon, and I'll be able to take it from him.*

As if The Razor is reading his mind, he steps back from the de facto fighting ring, and presents a placid posture. "Last chance, Tommy. Serve me unconditionally and reap the rewards of my number one. Say no, and I'll not only kill you, but your dear, sweet, picture-perfect family."

Tommy looks to the sky, "Dear God... I ask you not to judge me by the friendships I have fostered, but by the enemies I have fought."

Tommy leaps towards The Razor, feigning a wild southpaw punch. The Razor overcompensates and commits to the kill shot. The scepter, though a magnificent weapon, is a long, clumsy melee instrument, affording Tommy freedom of movement once he sneaks past the blade portion of the weapon. Driving inside, Tommy treats The Razor to a little Tommy Two Step, yanking The Razor's long blade from his belt sheath, and ramming it up his belly as he jukes underneath The Razor's left shoulder. Leaving the eighteen-inch blade lodged in The Razor's stomach, Tommy takes advantage of The Razor doubling over and his newfound tactical advantage of being on his backside, by landing a flurry of rabbit punches to the vulnerable area of the kidneys.

Culminating his twenty-punch combo with a swing for the fences, roundhouse backed by the full power of the God-soaked brass knuckles, Tommy doesn't wait for The Razor to regroup, and immediately grabs his right arm at the wrist and punches his elbow, snapping the arm at the joint. The Razor instantly drops the scepter. Tommy reaches around The Razor, grabs the handle to the long blade protruding from his belly with his right, and turns it as he squeezes a one-armed bear hug on The Razor's mid-section with his left arm. The move shuts down The Razor's feeble attempt to escape his embrace. While Tommy holds both the knife handle and The Razor's love handle, bracing for a highly-coordinated countermeasure, The Razor offers only an observation. "I should have pegged you as Roosevelt guy..."

In one fell swoop, Tommy releases his left arm from his midsection, and spins him around using the knife's handle, yanking the knife from his gut upon the completion of The Razor's 180. Before The Razor can move his one good arm to cover the hole, Tommy bends down and picks up the scepter. The Razor looks at the scepter and then to Tommy. Stoic, The Razor shows no sign of anger, or sadness. The blank stare of a sociopath settles in as he deliberates the end game. A hollow cough, accompanied by a wince, tells Tommy all he needs to know: The Razor has mere moments before he dies of internal bleeding.

Tommy tosses The Razor's blade to the side. It clanks on the pavement, making a single spark, before becoming lost on the lawn. Looking over the scepter with one eye, while holding The Razor with the other, Tommy seems to contemplate more than just their circumstance.

"You got anything to say before you go to Hell?"

"Mother Teresa once said, 'We cannot do great things on this earth, only small things with great love.' I love what I do… and I do it for you…"

Tommy takes the scepter in both hands, while advancing the short distance between himself and The Razor. Ramming the scepter in his chest, The Razor stands remarkably steady, moving only his eyes. Tommy examines the wide-eyed killer before pulling the scepter from his heart, taking a step back in order to allow The Razor a free fall. The hitman falls forward like a log, crashing to the pavement with a thud and shudder. Tommy picks up his well-heeled foot and examines the blood dripping off of it. Clearly disgusted but relieved, Tommy turns on his heels with slumped shoulders and begins to limp off, only to abruptly stop dead in his tracks. Turning to The Razor, Tommy bends down next to his fallen foe, and gently rolls him over. His eyes still wide open, his lips separated enough to whisper, The Razor looks frozen in thought, not dead. Tommy brushes back his jacket and pulls out the bag containing Dunlop's balls. He holds them up and examines them in the star-studded cityscape. "Now, where can I find a good Provolone at this time of night?"

Tommy stands up abruptly, and walks off into the night, holding the scepter in one hand and Dunlop's balls in the other.

### *The End*

**Thank you for reading my book!**

**I hope you enjoyed reading this book half as much as I enjoyed writing it. I try to write as events unfold, as opposed to directing the action to a predetermined endgame.
My thought is, if I don't know what's coming next, how could you? Obviously, logic dictates reason, and there's a reason for everything in this story, even the nonsensical stuff.**

**Please visit me on Facebook and share your thoughts @ Facebook.com/TheHitmanFromHell**

www.HitmanFromHell.com

Feel free to send me an email at
Trel@TheAlienClub.com

Made in the USA
Columbia, SC
14 November 2017